The Dark See

Book Three: The Moleskin Cap
M. R. Williamson

WolfSinger Publications ⚘ Brackettville, Texas

Dedication

At seventy-seven, there are several reasons why I am still writing.

Dedication and love for the craft is fueled by my loving wife, Connie Louise Gordin Williamson. I also have speculative fiction publishers that have no equal. Tyree Campbell of Hiraeth, Carol Hightshoe of WolfSinger, and Allan Gilbreath of Pro Se have been invaluable in that direction. Being human, I have had my lows, but my wife has propped me up, dusted me off, and handed me back my pen every time. Now, as I continue to look to the future, I have set three more possibilities in my path—the second book of 'Bridges Into the Imagination', third book of 'Moleskin Cap', and another, possible 'Horned Jack'. All three of these are already written, but need formatting and editing.

Just remember…you keep reading and I'll keep writing.

M. R. Williamson

Table of Contents

Introduction

Helen Durkin's adventure continues as she seeks to bond with the Wizard Andsell Phagan. With the help of his daughter, Prentis, she sees an easier way than she expected. But, as Fate would dictate, another is watching, and awaiting a time when Helen seems weak. Pragamore, now well up in his years, still watches from the forests of Phagan's Rift…

It is worthy of mention here that some of the characters within this story are ones from the previous novels, 'Pragamore, A New Beginning' and 'Krypendorf, the Fourth Lesson'.

Part 1

'The Return of James Torrance'

Staring into the eyes of a Dragon, only a breath away, would intimidate most anyone, human or not. But, somehow, Helen remained more curious than afraid. Perhaps the sixteen-year-old, strawberry blonde thought it was one of the visions she had when she first touched the dragon, only moments ago. In what she eventually considered, a quick glimpse into the future, she was certain she was flying with the dragon in the dead of night and over some vast body of water. But when she leaned over and looked down at the water just a few yards below, the only reflection she could see in the lake was that of the dragon.

Quickly backing away from the huge animal, she rubbed her eyes then watched Pren tighten the cinch on the dragon's saddle. But for Helen, everything right now was excitedly new as the smelly, leather saddle old Phagan's daughter was working on. But even that wasn't as exciting and intimidating as the creature only a few steps away and he was looking right at her. Just like a little bird staring into a great snake's eyes, she froze as she saw her reflection in his great, black pupils. Then, in the blink of an eye, she was back above the moonlit waters again with the wind rushing through her hair. The moon and countless stars, on a background of black velvet, seemed to be both above as well as below her. Leaning to her left, she looked along the neck of the great animal, but could not find the horizon.

~ * ~

"Helen!" a loud voice, that seemed to echo around in her head, called.

Helen rubbed her face and looked at Pren, standing right in front of her. The wind was gone, as well as the lake and the night.

"Are you all right?" Borack Cliffspring asked. The red-haired senior dwarf of Phagan's Rift looked closely at her expression. His dark eyes mirrored the smile under his walrus-like mustache.

"I...I think so," Helen managed to say, brushing her shoulder-length, blonde hair behind her left ear. "I think I just had a dream. I was on Pragamore. It was dark and we were flying over a huge body of water." She looked at Pren. "I don't usually have dreams, especially in broad daylight."

Quickly looking about the huge, russet barn, Helen could tell she was still standing quite close to the stairway leading down to where the old wizard and his daughter, Prentis lived. The Rift, as the Wizard Andsell Phagan's home was called, was a two-level home built by the Dwarves for the Wizard Phagan. Cut directly into the crevasse of a cliff overlooking Lake Horn, it was located at the western edge of the forests of Dragon's Haunt, considered the home of the last Dragons of Whitestone Castle.

Helen's gaze slowly found its way to Borack. His smile widened; a gesture instantly reflected in his big, blue eyes.

"All right," Helen grumbled. "What's going on? You are as hard to get information out of as your brother, Broderick. Was it a dream, or wasn't it? Who's playing games with my mind?"

"Who but a wizard?" Pragamore said softly as he eased up behind Borack.

Borack nodded silently. "I believe it's called the 'Dark See', My Lady," Borack said. It's jus' somethin' wizards are able ta do now and then. "This bein' your first ride, I believe the Old One is tryin' ta help ease the blow as it were."

"Indeed," Pren agreed, still smiling at Helen. "In his humble way, I believe he was, encouraging you. Did you enjoy it?"

"Very much," Helen admitted. "Why would he do that?"

"Why?" Pren laughed. "Who can understand the mind of a Wizard? As Borack said, perhaps he sought to encourage you. Now, let's see what you think of the real thing."

Helen looked toward Borack. He was standing next to the first stirrup of the saddle and holding out his hand toward her.

"You'll no regret it, My Lady," he said softly, with that same, friendly smile. "Just hold tight ta the saddle bar in front of you until ya learn ta relax a bit," he added.

~ * ~

Just minutes later, the great dragon was in the air and soaring away from Phagan's Rift. It was just after dusk, but the glow in the west was still holding.

Helen caught what she could of her breath and then tightened her grip on the saddle bar. Remembering her dream, she slowly edged close to the left side of the saddle and started to look down. But as she did, the great dragon jolted, sending her right back to the middle of the saddle.

"Well, this feels safer," she said as though relieved.

But, just as soon as she said that, something in front of her, and just above the saddle bar, began to glow. About eighteen inches across, the soft glow hovered in front of her, seemingly not affected by the wind. But as it hung there, floating between her and the Dragon's head, a face began to form within the glow. Framed by a full head of gray hair and broad smile, a plainly visible pair of bright blue eyes seemed to be looking directly at her. Then, just as suddenly as the apparition took form, it was quickly blown away like so much steam from a teapot.

"Phagan?" Helen's question was more of a thought than spoken word, but it was heard none-the-less.

The Dragon glanced back at her. "Your senses are improving, My Lady," he said softly. "He's been with us for less than a minute, yet you have already become aware."

Helen leaned forward, tightening her grip on the bar. "Is he testing me, Pragamore?" she said loudly, for the wind seemed to muffle her words.

"I am not sure, My Lady," the dragon answered. "But, since he's gone now, I would venture to say yes. You must exercise that talent, My Lady. It is a rare one indeed."

"Talent?" Helen slowly settled back in the saddle. "You mean being able to hear and see others who are not with me?"

"Exactly, My lady," the dragon replied. "You should learn the Wizard's ways if he will allow. The knowledge he is willing to impart would be a great benefit to you."

Helen quickly looked all about her. The dream was correct. The stars seemed to be all around her and no hint of a horizon save where the sun's glow was still lingering. That slight, yellowish glow was where the dragon seemed to be headed and it puzzled her somehow."

"Where are we?" she finally asked.

"We are off the lake, and headed for Whitestone Castle, My Lady. Are you cold? The clouds are back and the air seems full of moisture. Getting wet in April would not be good for you."

"I'm fine," Helen said. "Andsell loaned me a really nice coat. It's lined with fur and has a wind and waterproof outer layer."

Pragamore glanced back again. "Be that as it may, My Lady, it would be wise to move away from the clouds and head back across the lake. Too much of this night air could prove harmful to you. You are not used to it yet."

"Yet?" Helen smiled at the more-to-come statement. "My face is a bit numb, but I don't feel cold. Let's do go back across Lake Horn. I want to check something."

"As you wish, My Lady," the dragon replied as he banked to the right and then proceeded to glide in an easterly direction.

The treetops below passed under the Dragon so fast, Helen could hardly focus on any of them. In the distance, she watched the moon's light dancing upon the still, black surface of the lake. Approaching it very quickly, the ground seemed to give way to the stars as the horizon completely disappeared.

Just like in the dream, Helen thought. *I wonder...*

Once again she tightened her grip on the saddle bar and slowly leaned to her left. The dragon's wings were softly rowing now, and as timely as the pendulum upon her grandfather's clock. Looking down, she could still see the stars as well as the dragon. The smile upon her face widened as she noted herself atop the great creature.

"I feel your fear, My Lady," Pragamore said. "It is slowly waning from you, I think. Richard was very much like you—somewhat jaded, but fearless none-the-less."

Back to the saddle, Helen looked along the neck of the dragon, toward another, soft, yellowish glow in the distance. "Is that Phagan's Rift?" she asked loudly.

"It is, My Lady," the dragon replied. "But something is amiss. A lantern has been put in the great window."

Noting Pragamore was now veering slightly to the left and more northern, Helen leaned forward once more. "Is that some type of signal, Pragamore?" she said loudly.

"It is, My Lady. It means danger," the dragon explained. "We must go to Second Choice. We must not go to the old barn right now."

"What is this, Second Choice place?" Helen asked.

"It is the Stronghold of the Dwarves from Leachenwood, My

Lady," Pragamore said. "Those who have left Leachenwood, now live there and help the old wizard and…"

The dragon's comment faded off into the wind.

"You?" Helen guessed.

"That is correct, My Lady," the dragon replied.

~ * ~

In just minutes from the northern turn, the old dragon's wing-beats increased. Slowly climbing up and over the northern edge of the cliff, Helen gripped the saddle bar and then stood up in the stirrups. The second rise, now directly in front of them, didn't seem to be part of the cliff at all, but a steep formation of its own. Grass, rocks, and huge stones formed a sheer face that outlined some sort of cavern seemingly carved directly into the face of a small mountain. Made of wood, glass, and stone, the opening looked to be an entrance into a vast cavern. Yawning, like the mouth of some great beast, it looked to be forty feet tall and at least twice that wide. Dimly lit, it gave hints of several someone's standing within its shadows. Helen settled back to the saddle again as Pragamore gently dropped to the grass below.

"Second Choice?" Helen's question was weak as she strained to make sense of the dark silhouettes within the cave.

"Dwarves, My Lady," Pragamore said, holding his ground as one emerged from the cave and slowly walked toward them. His gate and direction showed he didn't fear the Dragon at all.

"Good evening and welcome," the little man said.

Somewhat loud and far too close, he looked to be the size of her friend, Bo Bumpus. Four to five feet tall, heavy set, and about sixty years old, as the world would judge men, his long brown hair was tied back tightly in a ponytail that reached down his back to the back to his belt.

"Good evening," Helen replied as she looked at the little man now standing close to the dragon's left wing.

Now, with a better look at who was atop the dragon, the Dwarf quickly removed his hat and bowed slightly. "My apologies, My Lady. I was of a mind that you knew."

"My apologies as well, My Lady," the dragon said, glancing back at her. "Second Choice is Leachenwood Two and my shelter when not at the old barn."

"Harskin Truft," the little man introduced himself. Stepping a bit closer, he held his hand up toward her. "May I help you down?"

Helen quickly released the front and rear tethers, slid a little from the saddle, and then took his hand. As she did so, she noticed two others approaching with lanterns.

One, looking much older, held his lantern high. The tips of his mustache meandered down his long, red beard to disappear somewhere there within. "And just who do we have here, bold enough to ride a dragon?" he asked.

"Bright Helen," Harskin announced proudly. "Who else would be upon the great beast?"

The two Dwarves quickly doffed their hats, bowing slightly.

"Why didn't ya say so," the young Dwarf grumbled, frowning at Harskin. He looked at Helen with a slight bow. "I am called Bitterthorn, My Lady. I am but an archer here at Leachenwood Two. This lad to my left is the archer, Dullbrier. You may already know of him as well."

Helen's smile widened as she paused, looking at the dwarf. His big, bulbous nose looked like an Easter egg, hiding in a nest of long, reddish-brown hair and mustache. "I have certainly heard of you, sir. Bo spoke of you several times. He is my closest friend as well as the first dwarf I have ever met."

Dullbrier bowed slightly. "He spoke of your meeting at your grandfather, the Doctor's place."

Pragamore looked down at Borack. "Why the lantern at the Rift?"

"Scar," Borack replied, watching the dragon's expression closely.

Although Pragamore said not a word, most all there noted he had begun to plow small furrows in the ground with his front talons.

"Now, Pragamore," Borack started. "You know we—"

"Should have drowned him," the dragon grumbled. "He's threatening everything I live for—just like the Witch Ibenus."

"Now-now," Dullbrier said. Nervously stroking his short, russet beard, he edged closer to the dragon. "You don't wan 'na end up like Bitterthorn do ya? His days were almost ended by evil as well. If it wasn't for a potent Bo made from your blood, he wouldn't be here with us today."

Seeing this, the other two Dwarves slowly backed away with Borack gently pulling Helen along with them.

Pragamore, now as quiet as a church mouse, slowly swung his head to face the approaching dwarf.

Dullbrier, sidling a bit more to the front of the dragon, held tight to his hat and smiled.

"Dullbrier…" the dragon started.

"I am here," the Dwarf replied, waving slightly.

Seeing Dullbrier release his hat, Pragamore blew a hot torrent of air, sweeping the hat from the dwarf's head. "If I find one more green, or any other color, grass snake in my hay I will feed it to you, you overgrown chipmunk. Now take our Bright Helen into the hold. Give her food and drink if she's hungry." Saying that, the dragon slowly turned, and once again, looked to the south, toward the Rift.

Dullbrier quickly stepped closer. "Pragamore…"

The old dragon slowly turned and squinted at the young dwarf. "Are you still here?"

Dullbrier nodded slightly. "Please, do not go anywhere tonight," the dwarf said. "The Faes of Kiendom have located that wicked man. They say he has others with him."

"True," Harskin said. "The Faes say he dabbles in the black craft. He could have the power to bring the end of your days. Please, stay the night with us and I'll personally kill you a young deer in the morning."

Pragamore glanced at Helen. "I am somewhat tired, the night is getting rather damp as well, and I don't cherish the unfriendly forests south of Phagan's Rift. Besides, the deer seem to run much faster than they used to."

"Good," Dullbrier replied, looking somewhat relieved. "The Faes say the name of your nemesis is James Torrance. Old Phagan says he practices the black craft as well."

"He's a sorcerer!" Borack exclaimed. "We should have not a thing to do with him!"

"Everybody just calm down a bit," Helen suggested. She turned to Dullbrier. "Who is watching this Torrance fellow right now?"

Dullbrier shrugged. "The last time I heard, just yesterday, it was Lilly Ann and Rosebud—Faes from Kiendom. They say he's just south of Clear Creek and quite near the Green river." He looked at Pragamore. "That puts him not far southwest of where John and Trudy Schmidt live with their daughter, Elisa at the main house. I find little comfort in that."

The dragon slowly looked south once more. "Very well," he finally replied. "Please take our Helen below and out of this damp air."

"I will," Dullbrier replied. Turning toward Helen, the Dwarf held his right hand out toward the cavern. "It's not as gloomy as it seems, My Lady. Allow me to show you." He turned back toward the dragon. "You are staying here for the night?"

Pragamore nodded a silent 'yes'.

Toward a very dim, amber light, Helen walked with Dullbrier into the yawning mouth of the cavern. When they reached the back, Dullbrier turned to his left and led Helen down a hallway lined with oil lamps every twenty feet. At the end of the hallway, and after stepping down a short stairway, Helen spotted a rather large and dimly lit alcove.

"Horses?" Helen asked. "I smell them and hay as well."

"Ya like animals, Bright Helen," Dullbrier said. "I know that.

Stopping just outside the alcove entrance, he stared at another dwarf, working the stalls. Seemingly irritated at having to stop his labors, the old dwarf slowly turned, pulled at his long, gray mustache, and then stared silently at Helen. Big, bulbous nose and no beard, he looked to be at least in his seventies.

"Smythe Stapin," Bitterthorn said. "He's our herbal physician as well as the closest thing to a vet we have."

"What's she doin' here?" he grumbled as he pulled out his long-stemmed pipe.

"Mind your manners, Grumpy," Bitterthorn said. "This is our Bright Helen. She just came in on Pragamore."

The old dwarf's eyes grew big as he froze with his pipe and tobacco pouch in hand. "Bright Helen? The dragon's here?" He quickly put his pipe and pouch back in his jacket and walked toward the three at the entranceway. "My apologies, My Lady," he said. "Is the dragon doing well? I mean, uh, you think he's feelin' all right?"

"A bit tired, but in good spirits, I believe," Helen replied. "Do you take care of him here?"

The old dwarf slowly nodded, his deep brown eyes still studying her. "He's like me, My Lady, too long in tha tooth. You should watch 'em closely when he flies. If he seems winded, get 'em down quickly." He looked back at Bitterthorn. "Now answer my question, dang ya. Why-is-she-here?"

Dullbrier shrugged. "Old Phagan had a light in the window. This is where Pragamore is supposed to come if he sees that, with Helen or not. They think Scar is somewhere about."

Smythe slowly nodded, still looking Helen over. "Tell me, Bright Helen, they call you an Entwhistle. That true?"

Helen's smile widened. "I can sense the presence of Druids, Mr. Smythe. Does that alarm you?"

Smythe nodded silently again, but didn't seem to be alarmed. "Guess not," he finally added, "Just like the Faes say—your aura truly must be bright after all."

"Why do they call him Scar?" Helen asked.

"Shouldn't speak his name, young one," Smythe grumbled. "But, since your new and all, I'll tell ya. The dark one was assaulting a young girl called Janice Dunn when the dragon chanced upon them in the wood not long ago. In the process of takin' him from atop the girl, the one called Torrance was gifted with a scar down the left side of his face, much similar to old Phagan's scar. That was gifted him by a Dragon as well, but under much different circumstances."

Helen nodded, looking past Smythe and toward the Shelties in the stalls on the far side of the alcove. "Do you live here as well," she asked.

"Uh," Smythe groaned as he wheeled and slowly walked toward the stall he was working on.

"Not here," Dullbrier whispered. "We all live below. Feel the breeze?"

Helen nodded. "Quite pleasant, really," she added.

Smythe motioned with his thumb toward the back side of the alcove. "Got'ta small fire room past that wall. It causes a draft that pulls outside air inside tha whole place below."

Helen, eased into the alcove, and saw a honey-colored pony in the stall Smythe was working on. "Is that pony yours? She's very beautiful. I've never seen a mane quite that long."

"They're all mine, Lass," Smythe replied with a slight smile. "The Dwarves ride 'em, but I own 'em an' take care of 'em."

Before Helen could say another word, there came a sound of some kind of disagreement echoing down the hallway from where they just came.

Dullbrier froze, listening to the shouts and loud talking. "That's our watch," he said excitedly. "Sounds like they've caught someone."

Immediately, Dullbrier led Helen back up the stairs and down the hallway; followed by Bitterthorn. As they neared the beginning of the hallway, they could see Harskin Truft arguing with another dwarf.

"Who is that?" Helen asked, pointing to a long-haired, red-headed, slightly portly Dwarf.

"Flagal Birchman," Dullbrier answered. "He's a bit of a hot head at times."

Quickening his steps toward the two, they both could see Pragamore had moved to the far side of the cave and out of the way.

"Flagal!" Bitterthorn squinted at the fat dwarf. "They can hear you clean down to the barn. Hold your voice down. What's got your dander up this time?"

Flagal threw the younger dwarf a slight scowl. "We should o' killed it!" the fat dwarf exclaimed. "Men have done for the Hobuerich, but we were left far too many o' their rides. Evil! All of 'em evil!" he added.

"What are you sayin?" Dullbrier asked with a slight squint.

"We…" Flagal paused, looking straight at Helen, now standing a little behind Dullbrier. "I beg your pardon, My Lady," he managed, quickly removing his hat. "I get a little passionate sometimes."

"What are you talking about?" Helen asked. "What rides?"

"Hagstorms!" Flagal exclaimed. "The Dwarves managed to poison the flock with tainted roastin' ears an' sweet feed, but a little one missed the feast. It was just born and couldn't eat with the others. Now, it's layin' as close ta its dead mother as it can get an' not a soul there can make a decision."

"Sick?" Helen asked.

"No, child," Flagal said. "It's just weak. I done said it didn't eat any of tha tainted corn 'cause it's too young. With its mother's milk now tainted, it will die eventually I'm sure."

"Take me to it," Helen said, stepping from behind Dullbrier.

Pragamore stepped closer, all but cutting Helen off from the others. He looked straight at Flagal. "Where do you have it?" he asked.

"Straight south of here, toward the old barn, and right on Clear Creek. He's quite near a great, white oak." Flagal replied.

The dragon quickly turned to Helen. "On me, My Lady. I know the place." His words were soft, but firm none-the-less.

"Uh…" Dullbrier followed Helen to the dragon's side. "You have two seats. Can I—"

"No," Pragamore snapped, looking straight at him. "You're almost as bad as was Bitterthorn—even if you are Bo's brother."

"Come on," Helen said. "What would it harm?"

"Uh…" The dragon slowly looked back toward the south. "All right," he replied softly as he gradually turned toward Dullbrier. "We'll swing by the lake and kick 'em off later."

After helping Helen to the first saddle, Dullbrier quickly climbed into the second and strapped in, front and rear tethers.

"Strap in tight," the dragon said. "This will be quick." He glanced back at the dwarf. "I'd hate for your falling off to be an accident."

Walking briskly from the cave, the dragon immediately took to the air, sending Helen and Dullbrier grabbing for the saddle bars. Three, powerful strokes and he had them well above the trees. Helen glanced back at the dwarf. His eyes were tightly shut.

"Open your eyes," Helen said loudly. "You can't see the beauty of it when they're shut."

"No…" Dullbrier slowly shook his head. "If I see, I'll fall."

"Way too late," Pragamore said. "The creek called Clear is but a breath away now. I can already see the huge oak in the distance."

Helen stood in the saddle and looked toward where the Dragon was headed. The huge white oak stood out plainly above the rest and as was said, it was quite near the creek. Gently circling it, the great Dragon swooped down and landed at a dead run, ending up right under the tree.

"Oh my," Dullbrier groaned. "Are we down? I think I'm gon'na be sick."

Ignoring the dwarf's situation, the dragon eased to the side of the great tree and then nodded toward those at the creek just an arrow's fly away. He immediately shook his head, clearing his nostrils. "Do not dismount, My Lady. The stench of death is strong here."

Dullbrier leaned to his right and looked around Helen toward the four Dwarves now standing at the edge of the creek. Even with the half-moon's light, it was clear enough to see several bodies of what looked to be horses. They were lying motionless on the ground, near the water.

"Stay in your saddle," Dullbrier said as he quickly unfastened his tethers. "I'll see what's goin' on."

Dullbrier eased from the saddle, down the three steps, and then walked briskly toward the other Dwarves. The closer he got, the more foul the stench became.

"Dullbrier, is that you?" one of the Dwarves shouted. "It's us—Theldon and my brother Grendrum Biardam! Galman and his son, Splinter are with us as well!"

Helen watched from atop the dragon as a young dwarf stepped from the group. Once away, he immediately broke and headed toward them at a dead run. Straight for the dragon he ran, not slowing at all. Pragamore slowly lowered his head to the child and shut his eyes for the hug he knew was coming. All of eight or so and three and a half feet tall, the sandy-haired dwarf grabbed the dragon's head just above his nose, and hugged him. He then gently pushed back to watch Pragamore's big, yellow eyes slowly open.

"Father won't let me go to the old barn," he finally managed. "I only get to see you when you come to L Two. Now, I am told, there are killers in the wood."

Helen eased from the saddle, smiled at the lad, and then walked toward the others at the creek.

"Who's on the dragon with you?" Grendrum asked, watching Helen approach. "And when did you get the courage ta ride tha beast?"

"That's Bright Helen," Dullbrier answered, ignoring the second part of the question.

"What's that awful smell?" Helen asked, holding her finger close under her nose as she approached.

"One of the last remembrances of the Hobuerichs, My Lady," Theldon answered, with a slight bow as he and the others doffed their hats. "I am Theldon Biardam, with my brother, Grendrum. Galman is with us and his son Splinter as well." He motioned toward the dead animals. "These are tha last of the Hags, My Lady. We have only the young one left. It would be as dead, but was much to young ta eat tha tainted corn."

Helen slowly stepped closer to the animals. Every bit as big as a full-grown horse, the creatures were a dusty shade of gray, with long, black manes, and stout looking necks and legs. All of their black eyes were open, but there was no movement from any of them. Then, she looked toward the creek. Another was lying there motionless, a mare. Just as close to her stomach as it could get, was the newborn filly. About the size of a young goat, it lay there watching her intently.

"Oh…my…God," Helen said weakly. Her voice soft as she slowly drew near the little one.

Theldon stepped closer. "We could kill it I suppose," he suggested as he glanced at Grandrum's son, Splinter, now standing close to Pragamore. "It would surely die anyways."

Helen shook her head. "That would be a poor testament to the compassion of Leachenwood would it not?" she said firmly. "Help me. We need to get it back to the barn as quickly as possible. It looks very weak. It's starving." She looked at Grendrum Galman for some show of compassion.

Smiling, Theldon slowly shook his head. "I see the Dragon's already rubbin' off on you, My Lady. He too has a way with strays and orphans as well. We already have two dogs, a goat, and a young fawn at L Two to take care of." He paused, looking closely at Helen's hopeful expression and then added, "I have a ground tarp I believe I can rig up if Pragamore will carry the creature and us as well." Theldon squinted up at her. "You do know this is a hagstorm do you not?" he asked.

"I know what they are," Helen replied. "But the little one we have here doesn't yet know just what she is, and she certainly doesn't know anything of Hobuerichs."

"Well…" Grendrum paused, smiling at Helen. "It seems you'll have the only hagstorm left. That is—if she lives."

"Yep," Theldon agreed. "If ya can keep tha wolf from eatin' it."

"Wolf?" Helen's jaw dropped a little. "Is Seleene in the forests again?"

Theldon slowly nodded. "There have been signs My Lady, and she is the only wolf in all of England. Now, she doesn't depend on tha witch for food. Ethrel Ibenus kept her well-fed—a gift from those other than tha English. She's been watchin' you at times. Noticed I did where she had made her bed. Spent tha whole night there she did while you slept."

The two Dwarves laughed. But Helen, looking into the green eyes of the young filly didn't acknowledge the poke.

~ * ~

Now, a good thirty minutes later, and with an 'all clear' on Theldon's cell phone, Pragamore took the three passengers back toward the old barn at Phagan's Rift. Being closer to midnight than not, the Dragon glided in, low over the huge oaks at the east edge of the barn. Landing softly in the grass, he then crept up to the front corner.

"Come ahead!" a familiar voice called.

Both Bo Bumpus and Borack Cliffspring stepped out of the dimly lit barn, smiling at the little group.

"Bo!" Helen exclaimed as she fumbled with her tethers.

"Where is Scar?" Pragamore asked as he stepped closer to the two.

Smiling at the dragon's concern, Bo reached up for Helen's hand. "Tha evil one left his camp in the wood some five miles or so south of here. There were two others with him shortly after eleven say the Faes. But he's not headed in this direction they think." Placing Helen's feet firmly upon the ground, he stepped back and smiled at her. "You had an unexpected place to visit didn't ya, My Lady?" he added with his eyes glued to Dullbrier.

"Uhhh…" Dullbrier glanced at Helen. "Bein' the air cold and damp, Pragamore brought her there instead of tha Rift. There was a lamp in the Old One's window."

"Uh huh…" Bo looked to Helen. "Bright Helen, I would ask you to keep L Two and its location a secret if you will. We believe the forests of Dragon's Haunt will last a bit longer than Old Richard's spell that protects us as well as Leachenwood.

"I will," Helen replied. "Would you please inform Pren we need Dr. Johnathan's help as soon as possible?"

Dullbrier eased the folded canvas down to Helen and she lowered it gently to the grass.

"His wife, Trudy, loves animals as do I, Bo," she said as she eased the corner of the canvas back.

"Bless-my-beard!" Bo took a step back and glanced at Borack. "Do ya know what that thing is?"

"A hagstorm," Borack answered weakly.

"No bad comments," Helen said firmly. "Right now, she doesn't know just what she is and we'll all help with that." She looked at Bo. "Go now, Bo! The rest of her family have been killed! She is starving! Go!"

As Bo headed for the UTV to fetch the vet, Helen looked at Borack. "Go and get Snowball. She is about to foal and I hope she has milk."

"Uh…me? Milk a—"

"Go!" Helen ordered. "I don't want her to die on me!" Helen knelt beside the filly and looked up at Theldon. "Help me carry her inside. This is as good a reason to stay here a while as any."

"I swear," Borack said, heading inside with the dragon right behind him. "I swear," he repeated as he glanced back at Pragamore. "Are you smilin'?"

"Dragons don't smile," Pragamore managed to say. "But, I cannot say I am not pleased."

~ * ~

Twenty minutes later, Trudy, Johnathan, and Bo pulled up to the open doors of the barn in one of the UTVs. Their daughter, Elisa, a fair-haired twenty-year-old, had joined them as well.

"Why all tha lights?" Bo asked. "Tha place is like daytime in here an' it's almost one in tha mornin'"

Borack stepped from the barn, pausing at the green UTV. "Helen's got tha little one drinkin' goat's milk she has. It's looking better already I think." He glanced back at the loft. "The Faes are here from the wood." He raised his eyebrows. "I don't think they're none too comfortable with Bright Helen's guest."

Johnathan quickly stepped from the UTV. "And this creature is a what?"

"Well…" Broderick led the group to the nearest stall and slowly opened the door. Wincing, he scratched the back of his neck as he looked back at Trudy and Johnathan. "Guess you could say it's kind of a dull, dusty colored horse kind-a-thing."

"My word," Trudy managed, staring at what Helen was bottle-feeding in her lap. "I've never seen an animal quite like that." She looked closer at the little filly, chewing on the bottle of goat's milk. "It has fangs?"

Borack slowly nodded, glancing up at the restless Faes in the rafters. But before he could comment, Phagan stepped from the elevator doorway and stopped, looking up at them as well. Janice Dunn eased from behind him and stood close to Dullbrier.

"Quiet!" The old wizard's voice was so loud it made them all jump. Phagan moved to Helen's stall and looked down at the two sitting in the hay. Gently placing his right hand upon Helen's head, he looked up at the Faes now gathering in the rafters right above them. Slowly shaking his head, the old Wizard said, "How is it that the very ones who keep civility in the forests of Dragon's Haunt have now, seemingly, lost their compass?"

Then, just as if a wave of shame had washed over them, the Faes grew very quiet, staring at the old, white-bearded wizard.

Lilly Ann, one of the oldest leaders of Kiendom, flew from the group and landed upon a rafter directly above Helen and the old wizard. "Does not the creature you are feeding represent the Hobuerich as well as the evil they perpetrated upon us all?"

"It-does-not," Helen replied loudly.

"Well said," Phagan added, never breaking eye contact with Lilly Ann. "I dare say that at the stage of its life right now, it knows only of what it needs, what it sees, and who helps it. And to shame one so little as this is, in my opinion, shameful to a degree, until now, previously unseen by me." The old wizard slowly looked at the thirty plus Faes now quite silent in the rafters. "All of my days, I've heard of the magic of the Faes of Kiendom and their glamour. You have seen something special in Helen, as have I and Pragamore. So much so, the dragon has made a pact with her. I have pledged my remaining days to educate her and bring to light the power hidden deep within her being." He paused, looking at them again. "Why don't you all do something for her—perhaps something that would open your own world to her a little? Would that be too much to ask?"

The Faes grew strangely silent, slowly looking from one to another. Then, ever so slowly, Rosebud lifted from the rafters just behind Lilly Ann, and floated gently down toward Helen and the filly. Barely able to hold its head up, the young hagstorm stared wide-eyed at the glowing creature now holding her hand out just inches from her nose. All of a sudden, the brightness that seemed to be gathering about the Fae, shot from her hand to the hagstorm's forehead. With that, the next, nine Faes, followed Rosebud's example, changing the filly's dull coat to a glossy black. The next ten, one by one, visited her and erased the bony, hard-ribbed appearance to one of a thoroughbred. The next ten brought the strength and health of one befitting its age. But now, all eyes were on the last, little Fae. It was hovering a good five feet above Helen and the filly. Young, seemingly twelve-years-old, the little, blond-headed Fae's countenance was enhanced by a bright, white dress. Looking confusedly at the beautiful filly now standing in front of Helen, a smile slowly formed upon her angelic face. Floating gently down in front of the little filly, she slowly placed her hand upon its forehead. Suddenly, and with a blinding flash, the brightness of the dress shot to the little Fae's hand and then to the filly's forehead.

"My God," Janet said weakly. "It left a four-pointed, white star."

"Yep…" Lilly Ann said. "That's the symbol of a gift from the Faes.

Old Phagan's eyes grew wide, looking at the little Fae, still hovering in front of the filly. But now, her dress was a dull, sandy yellow.

With a smile on his wrinkled face, the old wizard slowly held out his right hand toward the little Fae. Noticing the gesture, her eyebrows slowly raised.

"Come here, little one," he said softly. "I have a gift for you."

Slowly turning, the little Fae drifted to within a short reach of the old wizard and then stopped.

"What is your name, little one?" Phagan asked.

"Hopian, Sir," the Fae replied.

Phagan held his smile. "Such a selfless gift should not leave one so diminished. The old wizard gently blew across the palm of his hand toward the little Fae. Instantly, the drab sandy-yellow of the dress blew away like so much dust. It left in its place a brilliant, buttercup yellow.

Phagan squinted at the little Fae. "Could it be that one so young could be so smart to think of such a gift?" He glanced at Helen.

Hopian smiled. "For Helen," she finally said, and then flew back up to the rafters to join the others.

"For Helen?" The old wizard slowly turned toward Helen. She was smiling at the now beautiful filly standing in front of her.

"Hopian. That is a good name for your new friend." Phagan smiled at Helen. "That means one who always brings hope to others." He nodded toward the filly. "But, the gift she refers to is for you, My Lady. Now, just place your hand upon the filly's forehead right over the white star."

Helen's chin slowly dropped. "Oh no," she groaned. "The last time I did something like that, I woke up on the ground."

"Well," Phagan said with a chuckle, "I see you're still with us. This should benefit you greatly."

"All right," Helen said reluctantly.

She slowly rose up on her knees and placed her right hand upon the filly's nose. The young Hag closed its eyes as though enjoying the moment. Ever so slowly, Helen slid her hand up toward the white star upon its forehead. Then, true to form, just as soon as her fingers touched the star, darkness engulfed her world again. She never felt the old wizard catch her…

Part 2
Kiendom

With the scent of cool, April rain in the air, Helen slowly opened her eyes. It was night. At least it looked like it was, and she was lying in the grass. That was obvious, as well as the call of crickets filling the air all around. Looking above her, the dark sky was studded with more stars than you could count. They seemed so close you could almost touch them. But, as she watched, a particularly large one seemed to move—slowly, but move none-the-less. Realizing what she was looking at wasn't the sky at all, she quickly sat up. "It's the top of a cave," Helen whispered.

She looked about the strange place again, as she sat in the knee-high cool grass.

"Oh, my…" she managed as her gaze followed a little creek as it meandered around the stones and on deeper into what seemed to be another, huge cavern.

Little cabins of stone and wood bordered a bubbly creek at least forty feet wide. Each cabin was about the same size, but all distinctively different. Their windows, which had shudders, had no glass panes. Try as she did, she couldn't spot a chimney on any of them. Then, as she pondered the moss-covered roofs, she heard a soft giggle, quite near and to her left, but she could see no one at all.

Now, with the light of several approaching lanterns, her eyes were allowed to focus on one, particular person. The Faes, all of ten inches tall or so, wore a dazzling, white gown that seemed to reflect every point of light within the cavern. The procession, or so it seemed to be, looked to include at least thirty other Faes. Stopping about twenty feet from her, she saw a pure white owl glide over them and land between her and the others. Looking closer, she could see yet another Fae upon its back.

"Bright Helen!" the rider said loudly, as if announcing her presence. The voice was that of a young girl.

Helen's gaze still held on the lady wearing the white dress. She had long, yellow hair, and looked like someone's fairy grandmother.

Her blue eyes, even in the dim light, seemed to sparkle with life and excitement. Smiling, and with a slight bow, she said, "Ever since the dragon had us contact the Dwarves about his 'Special Someone', we have been wondering about you, Helen Durkin. But, true to Dwarf form, they have put action before clarity thereby bringing us to this point in your life.

"Feathers' Foot," the lady said, waving the now too close owl and his rider away a bit. "Your time is not yet."

"Do you truly ride the big dragon?" a little voice quite near and to her left asked.

Helen turned to see a little girl of perhaps eight or ten years old standing two paces from her. About four feet tall she appeared to be. Her pale blue, gossamer wings fluttered now and then with excitement, emphasizing her smile. She waved her hand in front of her and toward Helen. The dizziness that took her quickly brought Helen's hands to her face. Shaking the strange feeling from her, she looked back at the little, winged girl. The young Fae's smile widened, but without words.

"Hopian?" Helen managed weakly.

That is enough, Hopian," the lady in white said. "We must not keep Helen long."

"I know you," Helen said to the little girl. "You were one of those who helped me with the filly." Helen looked to the lady in white. "But now, you all are as big as regular people."

The lady in white smiled again. "Perhaps it is your size that is different," she said, keeping her place in the grass.

"My…size?" Helen saw, the Faes, now a little closer to her, were indeed her size as well.

"I am Fatae, the Queen of the Woodland Faes," the lady in white said. "You are in Kiendom, our home. It has been brought to my attention by some that we should provide aid to your particular situation. The Wizard Phagan has vouched for you and that is all I need. The Woodlands will provide at least two—"

"A-hem!" Hopian cleared her throat, holding her position quite close to Helen.

Helen turned to see Hopian holding up three fingers toward the Queen.

"She's a sprite," whispered a voice, so close to Helen it made her jump.

Turning in the direction of the whisper, she could see Rosebud and Lilly Ann only a short reach away.

Helen looked at Queen Fatae. "And the little one?"

"She is a sprite, but we'll watch her," Rosebud said with Lilly Ann nodding her approval.

Queen Fatae slowly shook her head. "She is head-strong, opinioned, and apt to cause much mischief at times. You will have your hands full, even for Faes."

The sprite and the two Faes slowly bowed.

"We will do our best, My Lady," Lilly Ann assured the Queen.

The Queen approached Helen with her wand out.

"Oh…" Helen said softly, seeing the bright blue gem at the tip of the wand start to shine brightly.

The Queen's smile widened. "Those three are now given the charge of 'Watchers' for Helen the White. That will make four, counting the dragon."

As the wand was held above her head, Helen felt herself being pulled from those around her and into a place so dark she could see nothing at all. The feel of the grass was gone and so were the rippling sounds of the creek as well as the songs of the crickets. For an instant, there was only darkness. But gradually, the scent of hay presented itself as well as the strong arms that were now holding her.

"Enjoy your trip?" a familiar voice asked, slightly above her.

Gradually opening her eyes, she looked up at Phagan's smiling face. Seeing others were now gathering closely about her, she tried to get up.

"No-no-no," Johnathan said. He lifted her from the old wizard's arms and set her feet upon the barn floor. "Take it easy now. You've been out for almost an hour."

"Out?" Helen slowly looked at those about her. "I'll say I have and how or where I went I'll never understand."

Pragamore eased from his stall in the rear of the barn and paused but a step away from Phagan. "Did the gift of the white star take you to Kiendom?" he asked looking at Helen.

Helen slowly nodded. "It did. I was told that is where the Woodland Faes live?"

"It is," a little voice replied from the dragon's head.

Squinting past the glare of the lanterns, Helen could see Rosebud, Lilly Ann, and Hopian, all sitting in the long, greenish-brown hair between the Dragon's great horns.

Helen smiled, looking at the dragon. "I see you've acquired new friends," she said softly.

Pragamore rolled his eyes. "An unforeseen blessing, My Lady."

Helen smiled, glancing at the little sprite. "We shall call the new filly Hopian."

The sprite quickly clapped her hands in approval.

"We have set up rooms for you and the Dwarves at the main house," Trudy said. "The Dwarf archer, Fairweather, has joined us. The filly, Hopian, will be fine right here at the old barn." Trudy smiled at Helen. "Your grandfather is at the main house as well. He was a bit concerned about you being away for so long."

"We'll be fine right here as well," Bo said. "Tomorrow, we will trek through the woods to L Two."

"Please stay long enough for breakfast," Phagan said. "Let us at least see you on your way with a full stomach."

"Sounds good to me," Fairweather agreed as he walked into the barn with a bit of a smile. "But we'll sleep in the third stall, close to the dragon if you don't mind. Some of us are a bit nervous in strange places."

~ * ~

The next morning, Helen awoke with the sun barely lighting the yellow drapes of her bedroom. Slowly sitting up, she looked about the room. The little wall clock showed 6:30AM.

"Barely five hours," she groaned as she looked out of her upstairs bedroom window.

"Helen! Are you up?" a familiar voice asked accompanied by a light knock upon her door.

"Uh…" Helen groaned. "I'm awake, grandfather, but just barely," she managed as she swung her feet to the cold, hardwood floor.

"Be quick," he advised. "The Dwarves are sure to leave early, and we'll want to go with Trudy in about twenty minutes to provide help with their breakfast. We'll then stay and eat lunch with Andsell at the Rift. He's quite excited about your first day with him. He's told me everything. Some of which is a bit hard to believe."

"Everything?" Helen quickly got up and grabbed her jeans from the nearby chair.

"Yes," her grandfather replied. "Your friendship with the

Dwarves and the Faes and you studying under him as well."

"Under him?" Helen hurriedly found her shirt and socks. "Have you heard from my father?" Helen asked.

"Well…" Her grandfather paused. "He has agreed to let you stay with me. Might best keep what is happening right now under our hats as it were, at least until you get a little older. Now, hurry up. Janice and Pren are waiting for us. We'll leave just as soon as you are dressed."

Realizing Bo was reluctant to come into the house of a man, Helen quickly put on her shirt, then searched for her shoes.

~ * ~

Just minutes later, on a cool and clear April Sunday morning, Helen helped Janice, Elisa, and Pren fill the breakfast basket for the Rift.

"Sleep well?" Janice asked, smiling at Helen as they loaded the two UTVs for the short trip through the woods.

Helen nodded. "So this is where the old wizard gets his supplies, food and such?"

Janice nodded with a bit of a smile herself.

Trying unsuccessfully to stifle a yawn, Helen managed, "Too much excitement and too little sleep. I don't want to miss Bo and his Dwarves when they leave for L Two."

~ * ~

In less than twenty minutes, Pren guided the lead UTV up to the old barn atop the overlook at Lake Horn. Seeing several Dwarves gathered at its open, front doors, she slowed dramatically.

"Has something happened?" Helen asked, taking hold of her grandfather's left arm.

"Not sure," Pren said. "They look both angry as well as afraid."

Pren slowed the lead vehicle to a stop. Glancing back at Janice, she whispered, "A scared Dwarf? Now there's something for the books."

Noticing Fairweather was walking toward them, Helen quickly got out. "What's happened?" she asked.

"We been set upon," the old Dwarf said. "Those workin' at Cherry Creek to bury the dead Hagstorms were attacked by Scar and two others as well. Men folk they looked to be."

"They took Grendrum's son, Splinter, they did." Dullbrier added.

"They don't believe much in the Faes," Fairweather said, "but they know they been watched anyways. Then they left in their smelly jeep thing. But that's not the worst of it, My Lady."

"No," Dullbrier said. "The Dragon's done left as well. Flew straight south he did, and madder'n a swatted hornet he was."

"Oh…my…God," Helen said. "Why would he do that?"

"They took Grendrum's son, Splinter, o' course," Fairweather said, a bit irritated. "Pragamore is quite partial to the wee lad." He then paused, looking straight at Helen. "This is not good, My Lady. Not good at all. No one knows how powerful Scar is. That halfling Elf may hold the power to finish the Dragon."

"I've got him!" a familiar voice called from behind Helen.

Quickly turning toward the barn doors, Helen could see Pren waving at them.

"We got the dragon spotted," Pren said as she waved excitedly toward the little group.

"How's that possible?" Fairweather asked as they all rushed toward the barn and followed Pren to where Andsell was standing."

"A laptop?" Helen chuckled, noting what the old wizard seemed to be toying with.

"Pren's contraption," Andsell said, staring at the little screen. "Complicated, but it does things I can't," he added, pointing to a red cursor on the screen.

As she looked at the little laptop, Helen noticed a small, blinking red light on what looked to be a map of the area they were in. "Are you tracking the dragon?" she asked.

Pren nodded. "We all watch out for the dragon here at the Rift, especially me and Flagal. I glued a small device between his shoulder blades while he was sleeping. Doesn't look like he's moving right now though."

Andsell scratched his head as he looked up at Helen. "He's fairly close to Cherry Creek I think." He looked at Pren and added, "We don't have the means to get there quickly and he's probably found them by now. Sorry, Helen," he added, looking back at the young girl. "Didn't expect to throw you into the fray this quickly. You are painfully unprepared and we have little time to address that I'm afraid. Do you remember the gift called second sight?"

"The Dark See," Dullbrier groaned. "Do we have ta go into the Neither with her right now?"

"Neither?" Helen looked at the old wizard.

Andsell smiled. "The Neither is something that some say is, perhaps, a bit on the dark side of magic. But, it is neither good nor evil unless you use it as such. Do you remember the gift?"

"I believe so," Helen said. "I remember Bo talking about it. Pren said I had a taste of it just before my first ride on Pragamore. It's a way of connecting with the dragon when I am not near to him. But…" She squinted at Andsell, "that's a wizard's thing isn't it?"

"Exactly," Andsell said. "Now, I want everyone to be perfectly quiet. Do you remember what appeared in front of you when you first flew with the dragon?"

"Yes," Helen replied. "It was you."

The old wizard looked at Dullbrier. "Shut the barn doors blow out all the lanterns, and then come and sit in the hay with us. But be as quiet as you can. It is before noon and we still have much of the day before us."

As the Dwarves scrambled for the doors and the lanterns, the old wizard took Helen by the hand. "Sit right down here with me in this nice, clean hay and close your eyes. You are a White, Helen. I pray this talent has vested itself with you, even for a short time."

As all took their seats surrounding Helen and the old wizard, he added, "Be very quiet now and let young White work."

Completely leery of what she was trying to do, Helen kept her eyes shut and listened for the slightest sounds from the others. Then, as she pulled from memory the face of the old wizard as it hovered between her and the dragon's head, a chilly breeze swept over her face. It was the same as the one she felt when actually on the dragon. But this time it was much different. This time it brought with it a sense of dread—anger, fear, and a sense of urgency almost possessed her. Quickly giving up on that feeling, she opened her eyes to check the others. But she saw nothing but darkness—one that had shut out all light and seemingly removed everyone from around her. As she pondered the reason for such a thing, Andsell's glowing face appeared about forty feet directly in front of her. Realizing she couldn't see the dragon as before, the vision quickly faded only to leave the sight of a river, winding its way before her through the woods. The sound of a waterfall could be heard quite near. What seemed to be a camp of three large tents was there as well with two men sitting near a small cook fire. As her eyes focused on the men, she noticed something peculiar just passed them and quite near the middle tent. It looked to be a four-foot square box made of three inch boards. The sleeping form on the floor looked familiar.

"Oh…my…God." Helen groaned as she rubbed her eyes. "It's a wooden cage!"

"What did ya see?" Fairweather asked.

The Dwarf's voice echoed through the trees above her like the wings of a flock of birds.

Removing her hands from her eyes, Helen could see Dullbrier relighting the barn lanterns. "I think he's watching them," Helen said. "And the little Dwarf is there. They have him in a wooden cage."

"A cage!" Bo cried. He looked toward Andsell with a puzzled look. "What must we do?"

"They're close to a river, quite near a little waterfall," Helen added.

"We must get there, quickly, before he has at them," Andsell said as he looked at Pren. "Where does that contraption say the dragon is now?"

"About two miles off the main road, quite close to Cherry Creek," Pren answered. "We'll have to use the UTVs."

"Leave now," Andsell demanded. "They are not on the island as first seen. Take Helen, Bo, Dullbrier, and the archers Theldon and Grendrum, Splinter's father."

Helen was pulled to her feet by Pren and Bo, then ushered out of the barn with Dullbrier close behind.

~ * ~

Helen held tight to the edge of the UTV's top as Pren barreled South on the forest road toward the main house. Still bewildered, not as much at what she had just seen, but how she was able to see it, she searched for answers in a place where not many were readily available.

Quickly passing the main house, Pren headed straight across the Windamere road and onto a smaller, sand and gravel road. Finally, as they drew near Cherry Creek, Pren slowed the green UTV and glanced back at Helen. She had her head in her hands and was very still.

Pren quickly stopped the UTV and placed her hand on Helen's

shoulder. "Are you all right?" she asked softly.

"It's too late," Helen finally said, sounding very scared.

Noting Helen's condition, Bo jumped from the second UTV and ran to Helen's side. "Are ya all right, My Lady? Did ya see somethin' else?"

Helen slowly nodded. "Yes, but I don't know what to make of it."

"Do your best," Grendrum said, now standing beside Bo. "I need my son away from those people."

"There was fire everywhere—tents burning, grass burning, and even the wooden cage was on fire." Helen grabbed Bo's shirt and then added, "There were two bodies on the ground! They looked charred and they weren't moving at all!"

"Not good!" Pren cried. She looked at Bo. "Get in and hold on to her. I'm afraid the Dragon's already had at them."

Pren stepped on the gas and off went the two UTVs again. Slowing as they neared the creek, she quickly came to a stop and turned off the engine.

"Right there!" Dullbrier shouted as he jumped from the second UTV.

Even without looking to where Dullbrier was pointing, all could smell the smoke from the burning wood. With it was a hint of something more pungent—death.

"Smell that?" Bo asked. "That's methane. Mixed with that wood smoke it is. Pragamore's fired up morn' once he has. This ain't good at all."

"Oh God," Pren groaned. "The dragon's really had at them. He's old. If he does it too often, he'll weaken and may not be able to fly for a while."

Not waiting for a decision, Bo jumped out and trotted southeast, along the creek toward the sound of falling water. His direction was now taking them away from the road and the UTVs.

"Here we go," Pren said as she, Helen and Dullbrier scrambled to keep up with the old Dwarf.

"Keep back and watch 'em," Grendrum advised, motioning for the others to slow a bit. "If there's anyone up ahead, he'll find 'em without bein' seen."

In what seemed less than ten minutes, Helen noticed Bo had stopped quite close to a small fir and seemed to be peeping around it. The fire, much of it just smoke now, looked to be about forty yards beyond him. Helen could see three bare, tent frames and the two bodies exactly where she was allowed to see earlier. One looked to be charred beyond recognition and the other doubled up into kind of a ball.

"Oh-my-God," Pren groaned as she trotted up behind Bo.

"We're too late to help them aren't we?"

"Dragon's gone," Bo said, almost disappointed. He nodded toward the charred, wooden cage. "Doors been ripped off and I don't see Splinter anywheres."

"Are the two on the ground dead?" Helen asked.

"Well…" Bo paused, looking at the demolished camp. "One's been reduced to a heap of shouldering cinders and the other's had his head pushed down into his rib cage." He looked back at Helen. "What do you think?"

All of a sudden, Grendrum broke from the group and ran toward the smoldering camp.

"Let 'em go," Bo said as he slowly followed Grendrum. "There's not a one here alive."

Pren slowly shook her head. "What now?" she asked weakly as she watched Grendrum desperately search the shouldering tents for his son.

"We need ta create some kind o' diversion, My Lady," Dullbrier said as he quickly looked about the burnt-out camp.

"Diversion?" Helen whispered as they followed the old Dwarf.

"Yep," Dullbrier said. "We got'ta get tha dragon out o' this, whole picture. If Scar can pin this on Pragamore, then others might just want to take a hand in the Dragon's demise."

"He's right," Bo said as he picked up an empty whisky bottle quite close to the campfire. "Find another bottle and we'll put a half-burnt rag in their tops and crack 'em at two of the hot spots."

Quickly working on Bo's plan, another bottle was found. One was placed at the campfire and the other at the wooden cage.

"Let's get out of here," Pren suggested. "This smoke is bound to attract somebody and they're probably on their way right now."

~ * ~

Now figuring, or at least hoping, Pragamore had Splinter, the four left the area as quickly as possible. At almost 1:00PM, Pren slowed the lead UTV as they approached the old barn at Phagan's Rift. The double, front doors were wide open. Several of the Dwarves as well as old Phagan himself could be seen inside with Janice and others.

"There's Splinter!" Dullbrier shouted. "The dragon's returned!"

Grendrum jumped from the second UTV even before it stopped. Stumbling at first, he ran directly to his son.

Pren and Helen quickly stopped the lead UTV just a few steps from the front of the barn. "How is Splinter?" they asked. "Was Pragamore with him?"

Phagan glanced at the young Dwarf. "He's none the worse for wear I suppose. The problem, I'm afraid, has now shifted to where the Dragon has gone."

"Is he hurt?" Pren asked, glancing at the others.

Phagan shrugged. "Didn't have time to see. He just flew in, put the lad down, and then flew off back to the north. Hardly said a word."

Pren squinted. "The north? What's he up to now?" Old Phagan looked at Bo Bumpus.

"Any number o' things," Bo replied. "Maidenhead, old home of Krypendorf the is there. It's also very close to the Valley of tha Dragons. Used ta be a good number of 'em back in the day. Not real sure 'bout that now though. Then, on north o' there, is Snow Mountain where tha Northern Elves used ta live. The castle is still there I am told, but don't know tha condition."

"That was over five hundred years ago," Dullbrier said. "Nothin' up there now but remnants o' things long past and ghosts."

"Yep…" Fairweather paused, looking at Helen. "Dragon said when the one called Constable comes an' asks 'bout who burnt tha camp, you can rightfully tell 'em he ain't here."

Pren looked to Splinter. He was standing very close to his father's side. "Did the bad men shoot their guns, lad?" she asked.

Splinter slowly shook his head. "They didn't have time, Ma'am. Pragamore came in so fast it was all over in less than a minute or so." A bit of a smile brightened his expression as he added, "He brought me right back here. I actually flew with him this time."

Pren smiled at the young Dwarf's excited expression. "Do you know the one called Scar?" she asked.

Splinter's smile instantly vanished as he slightly nodded. "He left before Pragamore came a-runnin'."

Old Phagan looked to Bo. "I've tried to connect with the dragon, but failed in the attempt I'm afraid. All I could see was the trees of some substantial forest. That could be any number of places." He glanced at Helen. "He's too used to me, Helen," he added as he then looked to Bo. "Take our Bright Helen to Russell's Beech at dusk and leave her there for four hours or so." Looking back at Helen, he added, "I know this is all new to you, my dear, but we're now between a rock and a hard place so to speak. I put an image in your mind when you first flew with the dragon. Do you remember it?"

Helen, still studying the uncomfortable look on Bo's face, slowly nodded. "It was your face between me and the dragon's head," she answered with a bit of a smile.

Old Phagan nodded. "You have made a pact with the dragon, Bright Helen. Of all the beings throughout history who have broken pacts, you will not find a single, symbiotic dragon among them."

Helen squinted. "Symbiotic?" she asked softly.

The old wizard smiled. "You wouldn't know that one would you?

Helen slowly shook her head.

Old Phagan's smile widened. "A symbiotic dragon is a wizard's dragon, My Lady. Pragamore once held a pact with the Wizard Richard Alvis of Whitestone. Whenever Richard itched, the Dragon would scratch. Now, he is yours. Once again, you must use the Dark See to help us find him and the sooner the better. He is up in his years and if he gets in trouble, he'll need a friend." He winked at Helen. "That bein' you."

Helen's eyes grew big. "My dragon?" she managed.

"Bo chuckled. "Did ya not hear, Lass? Ya made tha pact, Bright Helen. He is now yours and is very possessive ta boot."

"But what am I to do?" Helen's eyes narrowed at the old Dwarf.

"Dark is best," The Wizard Phagan replied. "There are fewer distractions. When you find the place, as before, you must close your eyes and think of my face between you and the dragon when you first rode him. Then, just speak to him like he was right there in front of you. Bo will help you with that later on this evening."

Helen instantly looked to Bo. His uncomfortable expression did little to help the moment.

~ * ~

Later that day, Bo took a UTV and drove Helen away from the old barn and toward a part of the forest she was unfamiliar with. To the southwest they headed and across the Green River where it was wide, shallow, and rocky. Helen watched closely. The trail they were on looked to be hardly used and dark was almost upon them. Bo smiled uncomfortably as he turned on the lights.

"There's that look is again, Bo Bumpus," Helen said. "You look worried, and more than that, you look scared. How am I to find comfort in that? What's going on now and where are you taking me?"

Bo rolled his eyes. "Ta Russell's Beech like tha Wizard said.

"I know this place," Helen said. "That is where Pragamore was born. What has this to do with anything? Why is it worrying you? We're going toward the Whitestone Trail. Why?"

Bo nodded. "So many questions," he grumbled. "We're about to pass Gray Rock. Grassy Lake is but a couple o' hundred yards to your left. We'll near the Great Beech just before we get to Gossimer Swamp. The Great Tree will be just past a little waterfall. You can't miss it."

"So…" Helen paused with a bit of a frown. "What has this tree got to do with me?"

Bo rolled his eyes again. "Everything, My Lady. It is older than both our ages and then some. It is where Pragamore was born. Remember? When that happened, some of the birth fluid seeped into the ground and eventually ended up within the tree itself. It has never lost a limb, My Lady, and doesn't seem ta know death. Your best bet to connect with the dragon will be alone and under that, big tree."

"Alone…" Helen peered out into the darkened forest. She was already feeling 'alone' somehow.

Just then, Bo slowed dramatically and eased the UTV into a shallow and rocky stream about twenty yards wide. Helen leaned forward. What caught her attention first was a huge, unreal, shadowy figure up ahead. Blocking out the stars, it loomed well above the other trees. As Bo eased the UTV from the far side of the stream, she could now see it wasn't a shadow at all, but the very tree Bo was speaking of.

"Oh…my…God, Bo," Helen groaned. "It's huge."

"Rightfully spoken, My Lady," Bo said. "Tha night is clear, tha moon is almost full, and we'll be under her in a minute or two."

Helen looked to her left at the moon's reflection off of what seemed to be great body of water. "Is that a lake?" she asked."

Hardly," Bo grumbled. "It's Gossimer Swamp, and a most uncomfortable place to be at after dark. Which is where we are at right now," Bo said. "A witch's paradise for sure."

"Witch?" The squint was back in Helen's eyes.

Bo smiled again. "Tha only witches here are in my memories, My Lady. But, all in all, this place still doesn't set well with me in any way."

"And where you are taking me does?" Helen asked.

"Not exactly," Bo grumbled.

Bo slowed the UTV to a stop and then looked slightly upward. "There she is," he added weakly.

"Oh…my…goodness," Helen said weakly as she looked also. "It must be at least two hundred feet high."

"Closer ta three," Bo corrected.

Helen eased out of the UTV, staring at what looked like snow in what little light the moon had to offer.

"Is that snow in April?" she asked, glancing back at the Dwarf."

Bo, joining her in front of the UTV, slowly shook his head. "Go take a look, My Lady."

Slowly easing more under the great tree, Helen knelt to her right knee and scooped up the tiny, white flowers. "They're blooms, Bo," she said weakly.

"Yep," the Dwarf answered. "Gon'na make a million beech nuts this year I'll bet 'cha."

"And Pragamore was born right here?" she asked.

"Yep, My Lady," Bo said. "His mother, Thumbra, lost her amniotic fluid close to the trunk on the south side. It has been recorded in the Tombs for all ta read. Tha Great Beech is over six hundred years old. I would say on its south side is where you should sit and use tha Dark See."

"I see," Helen said weakly. "Bo…"

"Yes, My Lady."

"I'm not a big fan of being alone in dark places, especially in a place like right here. Will you stay with me?"

"Alone…?" Bo laughed silently, trying to conceal it with his hands.

"Bo Bumpus!" Helen clouded up like a thunderstorm. "This-is-not funny to me. I am now in a world where I know much less than very little."

"Beggin' you pardon, My Lady," the old dwarf apologized as he tried to wipe the amusement from his expression. "The Old Wizard told me ta leave you here. But alone you will never be, My Lady. Do you not remember your 'Watchers'?" He then pulled his flashlight from his back pocket and shined it up into the great tree's limbs. "Where are you?" he shouted so loud it made Helen jump.

"Who are—" Helen asked.

"Over here," came a little voice, interrupting Helen's question and answering it at the same time.

All but speechless, Helen followed the beam of light from Bo's torch, she noticed flashes of color here and there, darting about the limbs way above her. There a bright blue, then a red, and very close, a brilliant green. Then, captured by Bo's torch light, her eyes focused on two, tiny figures sitting upon a limb barely ten feet above her.

"Lilly Ann? Rosebud?" Helen asked softly.

"Move that blinking light!" Lilly Ann exclaimed. The Woodland Fae was dressed entirely in shades of brown with her dress mimicking the leaves of the great oak. Unlike that FaeLilly Ann, Rosebud's dress more resembled the green leaves of the great tree itself.

Bo moved the beam to the left a bit.

"Why would you think a Wizard would EVER be alone?" Rosebud asked. "Did you not hear what the Queen said? Does 'Watchers' mean anything to you right now?" Rosebud stood there with her hands on her hips and stared down at Helen.

Helen slowly shook her head and smiled. "Perhaps you missed the 'different world' part," she finally got out.

"We did," Lilly Ann said. "But since you made a pact with the Dragon, he would never be too far away. "Did YOU miss Bo's 'very possessive' part?"

"Guess I did," Helen admitted with a slight smile.

"Except for now," Rosebud said. "I think he's left the forest 'cause that constable guy's comin'."

"Yep," Bo said. "The fire was turned in by a local who also found tha bodies. Tha law will be snoopin' 'round the area tomorrow I'll bet. You'd best do this thing right now," he added, nodding toward the trunk of the tree. "If you like, I'll build you a small fire."

"I'd like," Helen said, studying the darkness beneath the great tree.

Part 3
Along Came a Dragon

Helen sat with her back against the old tree and stared out into the darkness. It was 10:30PM by her watch and Bo appeared to be nowhere around. Although she knew the limbs above her were alive with Watchers, the glow from the little campfire did little to comfort her. She slowly pulled the blanket Bo had left her over her chest and looked at the little pile of extra wood the Dwarf had left. All she could think about now was the taillights of Bo's UTV as they left by the little trail that brought her here.

"What now?" she whispered to herself.

"First test," a girlish answer came from just above her.

Looking above her, she could see nothing—no movement or color as before. But then, she didn't have Bo's torch to help her.

"Call your dragon," another girl said from the darkened limbs way above her.

The laughter from someone above her garnered a sound slap on bare skin.

"Shut up, Rosebud," another snapped, sounding very much like Lilly Ann.

"But Pragamore's not here," Rosebud countered. "I have heard it said by those who should know. How can he hear her?"

Another slap echoed thought the huge tree.

"Ouch! Don't hit me!" Rosebud said.

"That's a fine show of support for a Kiendom Fae," another voice said from the darkened tree above her."

Just then, the sound of rustling leaves seemed to float through the air from above her. Knowing that to be a Fae's wings, she followed the sound as best she could. Her gaze ended up on the little pile of wood. There, on a small log atop the pile, stood Lilly Ann.

"What must I do now?" Helen whispered.

With a deep breath of disappointment, the little Fae cocked her head sideways. "Do you not remember what Old Phagan told you?" she asked.

Helen nodded slightly. "Close my eyes and call my Dragon."

"Exactly," Lilly Ann agreed, casting an angry glimpse at muffled laughter from the darkened limbs above them. "We all should know this is your first time, but have a little faith in the Wizard, My Lady."

"Well, it's worth a try," Helen mumbled weakly.

"Do NOT try," Lilly Ann grumbled. "DO or do NOTHING at all."

Without another word, Helen closed her eyes and thought of her first ride across the lake with Pragamore. Much to her surprise, the same, cool breeze presented itself raising chill bumps across her bare arms. Knowing there was not a breeze before, she could not only feel it, but hear it play with the flames on the campfire as well. Then, the scent of the new saddle presented itself as the breeze got so strong it was whistling past her ears. Wanting to take a peek and knowing she shouldn't, Helen put her hands over her eyes and held them tightly against her face. But the light broke through anyway, bringing the old Wizard's face a short distance in front of her own.

"Are you all right, My Lady?" a low and guttural voice asked very close to her.

Down went Helen's hands to the grass. Bracing herself against the ground and the tree trunk, she looked across the campfire and into a face she had seen many times before.

"I am fine, Pragamore," Helen said weakly as she wiped the tears from her cheeks. "I was worried for you and doubted myself as well. Did they harm you back at the burned-out camp?"

"Nothing that can be seen, My Lady," the Dragon answered. "But I fear my actions will bring prying eyes much too close to the Rift."

Just then, the sound of laughter came from above them. It was so out of place, Helen looked up just in time to see Rosebud tumble from her limb and fall onto a pile of dry leaves to the left of the campfire. Helen squinted back up to where Lilly Ann was standing. With her fists on her hips, the older Fae seemed totally disgusted with the younger one.

"Enough!"

The loud command from the Dragon made Helen jump as she watched him blow a torrent of hot gas toward the instantly smoking pile of dead leaves to her left.

"Yikes!" Rosebud squealed as she shot from the smoldering leaves toward the darkened branches above them.

Helen tried to follow the little trail of smoke, but it disappeared way up in the huge tree.

"That's-not-funny!" Rosebud called from the darkened branches above them.

"You're entirely correct," the Dragon replied. "Your actions are anything but funny today." He returned his attention to Helen. "What is your pleasure, My Lady?"

Helen instantly glanced up at Lilly Ann.

"Don't squish her yet," Lilly Ann said. "She might be useful later."

The Dragon raised his head sharply to look up at the little Fae. "I meant—"

"Oh…I know what you meant," Lilly Ann interrupted. "Rosebud can't help from being Rosebud."

"Please…" Helen slowly stood and brushed off her jeans. "Let's all go back to the old barn at the Rift. I'll be there just as soon as somebody can find Bo and tell him to pick me up."

"I'll go," Rosebud said, standing next to Lilly Ann.

"No!" Lilly Ann snapped. "Your clothes are still smoking. They'll flame up if you fly right now. Go find some water."

"I'm right here!" spoke a voice from the darkness to Helen's left.

Hearing the UTV start up, Helen smiled as she looked at Pragamore. "I'll meet you back at the Barn. Please be there this time."

"As you wish, My Lady," the Dragon replied and he was instantly off, not waiting for another word.

~ * ~

Just past midnight, Bo slowed the UTV to a stop right in front of the old barn's open, double doors.

Seeing that, Fairweather eased from the darkness, lighting his lantern. "Good evening', My Lady," the Dwarf said softly. "Most have left for L Two since the Dragon returned just a short while ago. Are all okay?"

"We are all just fine," Helen said.

"Very good," the old Dwarf replied. "Now, go and get some sleep if your excitement permits. We'll need sharp minds at work here tomorrow if the inspectors come callin'."

~ * ~

The following morning at the main house's breakfast table,

Helen's day started with a knock upon the front door. Easing the remnants of her third cup of coffee back to its saucer, she listened to Pren as she answered the door.

"Can I help you," Pren asked as she stepped out onto the front porch and opened the screen door. "I am Prentis Phagan," she added as she gestured for him to come onto the porch.

"Perhaps so," a voice that sounded like a young man in his late twenties or so replied.

"I am Constable William Hobie. I'm investigating the deaths of two campers sometime yesterday evening and not too far south of here. Have you heard anything about this?"

The young Constable looked past Pren and toward the dining area but could not see Helen where she was sitting. Hearing Pren hedge around the questions, Helen quickly got up and walked into the living room. Through the windows, she could see a black Volvo in the driveway. As she eased closer to the still open front door, she could see Pren on the front porch talking to the man. She stopped cold. He was trim, young, over six feet tall, and had dark brown hair. Brushing his hair back with his right hand, he paused, now, looking at Helen as well. His dark, brown eyes all but captivated her.

"Oh, I'm so sorry," Helen finally said. "I didn't mean to stare, but…" Helen paused, looking into those eyes again.

"This is our guest, Helen Durkin. Perhaps she can answer some of your questions," Pren said with a smile.

"Uh, yes," Helen said, trying to collect herself. "I didn't mean to stare," she repeated.

"That's fine," Constable Hobie replied. His smile widened. "Did you hear the questions?"

Feeling her face warm, Helen replied, "I did. One was burned you said and the other was…" Helen paused, almost painting herself in a corner."

"I didn't say." The Constable's eyes narrowed. "But, all in all, he was burned also. But the second man's head was driven down into his rib cage. Never seen anything like that at all. It had to be some-one with great strength to do such a thing."

Helen smiled, seeing Pren back slowly away from the door. The raised eyebrows and 'You've got him' look on her expression wasn't hard to read. "Looks like you know more than we do," Helen told the Constable. "Do you live near here?" Helen shut her eyes and rubbed her forehead. *Can't believe I just said that,* she thought as she looked back at him.

"Actually, I live a little east of Lake Horn, off the main highway. My father has a farm there and I live with him." He smiled at the girls again and then added. "I know just about every animal in these parts. But at that campsite, I found one, good set of prints. They were quite large, and don't match anything I've ever seen. Would you mind if I had a look around the house and barn?" He held his smile, looking from Helen to Pren and back to Helen again.

"Well…" Pren paused, glancing back toward the dining area. "This is not our place, but I don't think they will mind. Mr. and Mrs. Phagan are at their animal shelter and won't be back until somewhere around 6:00PM."

"I'll go with you," Helen volunteered, watching Pren's smile widen.

Pren instantly stepped back close to the nearest porch swing. "Have a happy hunt," she quipped as she winked at Helen. "Best watch the dark parts of the woods though."

~ * ~

Walking from the house, the two continued on up the paved road and toward the new barn. The Constable continually checked where the grass was thinnest, but came up with nothing it seemed.

"Still searching for this creature with big feet?" Helen asked.

The Constable smiled, pulling his gaze from the ground to Helen. "What did Mrs. Phagan mean by 'dark parts of the woods'?"

Helen shrugged, holding her smile. "Got to be some kind of Red Riding Hood thing I would guess. After all, this part of the forest was once called 'Dragon's Haunt', and strange things did happen here from time to time. But, all in all, that was a long time ago."

"Like…" The Constable's smile was still there.

Helen slowed as they approached the two huge barn doors. "Lions, tigers, and bears I guess." She grinned at him as she opened one of the big doors. *What am I doing? Pragamore comes in here as well,* she thought.

"Helen?" the Constable prompted.

"Yes?" Helen pushed the door open a little wider. "There you go. Not much light in there, but you can still try if you like. The barn's floor is dirt, but it's provided with fresh, clean hay, Mr. Hobie."

"Bill," the Constable said as he slowly stepped inside.

"What?" Helen asked.

"My first name. You can call me Bill if you like."

"Yes," Helen said. "I would like that."

"Do you raise cattle here?" the Constable said. "I see a ton of hay in here."

"I'm just a guest, Bill," Helen said. "But they do have a few head and some sheep I am told. Just for personal use I believe."

"I see." The Constable knelt and gingerly removed some of the dusty hay in front of him.

Helen could see two sets of holes in the hard dirt. "What's got your attention?" she asked.

Bill slowly shook his head. "Not sure. There are five holes here fairly close to one another and another set hardly two feet from the first. There seems to be thumbs here, directly across from each other. I would say claws, but even a big grizzly bear wouldn't be this large."

Helen stepped a bit closer. "Not sure either," she lied. "Perhaps one of their machines made it. They have rakes and windrows under the lean-to sheds in the back. They have funny, metal wheels. Besides, those are pretty big for an animal track."

Bill glanced at her as he slowly stood. "Lions and tigers and bears?" he muttered. "I would like to believe that, but these are all but a match to the ones I found at the burnt-out camp."

He pulled out his phone and took a picture. But just as soon as he did, he put his finger under his nose and squinted.

Certainly not puzzled by that expression, Helen could already smell the odor, and it wasn't cow manure.

"What in the world is that smell?" Bill asked, looking at Helen.

"Not really sure," she answered. "Smells like an outhouse crossed with gasoline maybe. There are two, old Ford, eight N tractors here as well."

Still guarding his nose, Bill slowly eased toward the back stall with Helen close behind. The gate was ajar, but not all the way open.

"Oh jeez," Bill groaned as he opened the gate a little wider. "What the devil is that?"

Looking to where he was pointing, Helen could see a six by ten-foot solid wooden box about three feet high. It was at least half full of a mixture of hay, dirt, and what looked to be coal black manure.

Helen slowly shook her head. "Don't ask me to explain that. Looks like some kind of compost stuff."

Easing a plastic bag from his jacket, the Constable searched about the floor.

"What are you looking for?" Helen asked.

"A stick or something," Bill replied. "I want a sample of that black stuff."

Picking up a small stick, he eased closer to the box. "I was raised on a farm, Helen. But I've never smelled anything like this. Cow manure doesn't look like this stuff, and the smell is mingled with methane I believe, and a bit more than usual."

Helen watched him put a small sample into the sandwich bag. Taking another sample with the stick, he turned and walked past Helen and toward the open doors.

"Come with me," Bill said. "Let's go outside. I want to check something."

As they walked out and into the fresh air, he turned and held out the stick with its black sample toward Helen. "Take this. I want to try something."

"Really?" Helen asked, looking at the foul-looking black matter clinging to the end of the little stick.

Reluctantly, she slowly took hold of the ten-inch stick and held it away from her. "What are you doing?" she asked, seeing him searching through his pockets.

"Watch," Bill said as he pulled out a Zippo cigarette lighter. "Now, whatever happens, don't move a muscle."

Bill flipped the lighter open, struck it, and then eased the flame close to the black matter upon the end of the stick.

"Hold still. You're backing up," Bill cautioned.

Doing exactly as she was asked, Helen watched the flame get closer and closer to what she knew was Dragon scat. Slightly closing her eyes and gritting her teeth, she continued to watch as the Zippo's flame neared the black matter. Then, as it got within three inches of the end of the stick, the black matter exploded into what would resemble a cross between a roman candle and a sparkler.

"Jesus!" Helen cried as she quickly tossed the flaming stick to the hay on the barn floor.

"I got it! I got it!" Bill said as he stomped out the flaming hay.

Bill, now in full Constable mode, looked back up at Helen. "Methane wasn't it? I thought so and you knew what it was. I could tell by the expression on your face. You knew it was going to flame up didn't you?"

Helen shrugged. Maybe you had best talk—"

"I'm talking to you, Helen Durkin," the Constable interrupted. "I've got two men dead and burned to a crisp by who or whatever makes this stuff and now it looks like you have all the answers. Now, I don't want to spoil our budding relationship, but if you don't give me those answers, I'll have to take you in. The High Sheriff doesn't have my sense of humor in cases like this and I don't want him to have to question you. Who owns this place?"

Bill paused, looking at his now scared and confused suspect.

"John and Trudy Schmidt," Helen finally managed to say.

"Earlier, they were called Phagan," Bill grumbled. "Do I have to go back into my Constable mode?"

"Trudy is a Phagan. My mistake," Helen said. "Like I said, they are both at their veterinarian hospital and boarding business. They like animals…all kinds of animals."

"All kinds?" Bill squinted. "The kind that makes scat like what we just found?"

The nod from Helen was only slight, but Bill noticed it none-the-less.

"You're not gon'na tell me what it is are you." It was a statement—not a question.

"I shouldn't," Helen said weakly. "If I did, you wouldn't believe me anyway and I'd end up in front of the Sheriff."

"Fine." Bill rolled his eyes, his gaze ending up outside the barn doors. "I don't want to see you there either. I'll just chase this rabbit toward the Veterinarians I guess."

~ * ~

Thirty minutes after the young Constable left, shortly after 10:00AM, Helen and Pren left the main house on one of the UTVs to join the others at the old barn above the Rift. The day was cloudless and the old, faded red barn was entirely shaded by the huge oaks that surrounded it. But instead of slowing as they neared it, Pren stopped about thirty yards from the front doors and sat there without a word.

"What is it?" Helen asked.

"Not that sure," Pren said. "Something is different, and I can't put my finger on it yet."

"You see something?" Helen asked.

Pren nodded. "Are you sure that Constable left our place?"

Helen shrugged. "Not that sure really. I know he was more than just a little suspicious when he drove off. He discovered tracks in the barn—Pragamore's claws I think. He also found where you guys put the dragon's poop." Helen smiled. "I was making good time with Bill, but when that poop flamed up like a sparkler, he went straight into Constable mode again."

"Bill?" Pren's smile widened.

"Well, he is terribly good looking," Helen replied with a wide smile herself.

"There it is again," Pren said, pointing toward the partially open doors of the barn.

Looking in that direction, Helen cold see a shadowy figure darting here and there past the open doors.

"Oh gosh," Pren said with a chuckle. "I think that's Snowball, Pragamore's goat. She's playing with someone I believe."

"Yes," Helen agreed. "A little girl I think. She couldn't be more than twelve and has a beautiful, yellow dress on."

Pren slowly shook her head. "I don't know a soul with a young girl in this area." She inched the UTV forward. "Where in the world did this one come from?"

Seeing the bright buttercups on the yellow dress, Helen's chin dropped. "That's Hopian," she said softly. "She is one of my friends. Actually, she is a Sprite. The Kiendom Faes rescued her from the wolf, Selene, some time back and raised her as their own."

Then, as the UTV neared the barn, another figure lying in the shady, back side of the open space of the barn slowly took shape.

"Pragamore is here," Helen said.

Pren stopped just ten yards from the barn's partially open door.

"He's lying down," Helen whispered. "Ease on up and we'll see what's happening. I'll bet old Phagan has something to do with this."

"You think it's all right to get close?" Pren asked. "He's been acting strange ever since that episode back at the camp."

"Sure," Helen said. "I would know if it wasn't."

"Very well," Pren said as she eased the UTV closer and then stopped just a short distance from the nearest door.

"Is it safe?" the dragon asked.

Helen nodded with a bit of a smile. "You mean Scar?"

Pragamore nodded.

"I suppose so," Helen answered. "Haven't heard from the Faes. Old Phagan has all of Kiendom watching him right now."

The old dragon slowly eased his head down to the top of his hands, resting upon the thick, yellow hay of his stall.

"Hopian! Hopian!" came the call to the left of them. Although the voice was familiar, Helen quickly looked for its owner, but could see no one.

Pren chuckled. "Over there," she said, pointing toward two, large cellar doors mounted on the floor at a forty-five-degree angle.

"I don't see a thing," Helen said.

"Look close," Pren advised. "See that copper pipe just right of the cellar doors?"

"The one protruding out of the wall?" Helen asked.

"That's the one," Pren said.

"Hopian! Hopian!" came the call again.

"Quick." Pren nudged Helen's arm. "The Wizard's on the other end of that pipe. Go and talk to him."

Jumping out of the UTV, Helen noted the little Sprite was doing more watching than moving toward her summons. Stopping just short of the pipe, Helen eyed the new, wooden, cellar-like doors. "Andsell!" she shouted.

"Helen?" came the acknowledgement from the old Wizard.

"Yes sir," Helen replied.

"Most are already here," Andsell advised. "We are awaiting our supplies. We have guests for dinner and the chickens are in the oven. Only got turnips. Is Pren with you?"

"Yes Sir," Helen replied. "And she has several bags for you."

"Check the dumb waiter," Pren said as she trotted toward the cellar doors.

"Dumb what?" Helen asked.

"This…" Pren quickly opened another, new looking, two foot by three-foot door mounted on the wall just to the left of the pipe.

Looking behind her, Helen could now see Hopian carrying the supplies from the UTV toward them.

Helen squinted at Pren. "This door carries things down to the Rift?"

Pren nodded. "The old Wizard had the Dwarves build the elevator. Bo put in the dumb waiter just for kicks. Worked out pretty well though." She paused and glanced at the Dragon. "I think Phagan knows Pragamore's days are numbered," she whispered "You see, the Dragon has been his only way to get up here easily. The steep stairs were beginning to hard on him." She smiled at Helen again. "You know, he's very excited you are coming.

"Everyone knew I was coming?" Helen asked.

Pren nodded. "He wants to test your abilities, Helen Durkin. Ever since the Faes started calling you Bright Helen, he has thought of little else. It would seem to me a person like you would want to train under one of the last, real Wizards. Would you not?"

Helen paused, looking completely surprised. "My word," she managed weakly. "It has come to this at last. I would like this very much, but I didn't know just how to go about asking for it."

"Well…" Pren nodded toward the Dragon's stall.

Looking closely, Helen could see Pragamore was watching them.

"You see, the one you're looking at, asked your question to the old Wizard not long ago," Pren said. "The answer awaits you right now down in the Rift. Shall we go?"

"We shall," Helen agreed as she watched Hopian slowly open the slanted doors.

But instead of seeing the usual steep stairs, she stepped down into a small room with wooden walls and floor that could easily hold six people or more.

Pren nudged her inside with Hopian right behind them. "Push that red button," Hopian said, nodding to her left.

Helen quickly obliged, and a motor from somewhere below them cranked up. With a small jar, the whole room slowly began its downward path causing the front wall to slowly move upward.

"Great Scott," Hopian said. "This certainly beats those steep stairs." She slowly turned to Helen. "Don't let the old one spook you. Remember every word he speaks to you, and for Pete's sake, don't say 'Wow, I can't believe this!' You'll get a lecture and a half."

"Does Andsell use the stairs at all?" Helen asked.

"Oh no," Pren said. "When you get down to the rift, look to your left. There's a door that goes right out and onto a huge platform outside where the Dragon lands. As I have said, from there, Phagan rides him to the top, or wherever he wants to go."

"Well…" Helen paused, seeing a light from another place was quickly presenting itself in front of their feet.

Then, as the elevator slowed to a stop, a huge room was open to them. Helen leaned a bit forward. The room was not like anything she had ever seen before. It was very large, at least forty feet wide, three times that long, and about twenty feet to the wooden, vaulted ceiling. The far wall was adorned with six-paned windows that extended from the floor to the ceiling. A huge, mahogany table sporting at least a dozen chairs sat in the middle of the windows. Looking through the windows, she noticed a huge patio that covered the whole front of the 'Rift'. It extended around to the left side of the room where a door awaited those who were brave, or at least curious enough to look. Huge, padded chairs and couches were in each corner of the room and along the walls.

Helen looked at Hopian. "I see your 'Dragon Walk,'" she said softly.

"Phagan! Phagan! Phagan!" The shrill shouts echoed in the large room as a large, red and green object shot across the ceiling to the right where it landed on a six-foot perch.

"A parrot?" Helen asked softly.

Pren laughed. "Not just a parrot. He's Apple, the Wizard's friend." She glanced at Helen, still pausing just inside the elevator opening. "You gon'na go or do we just stand here until someone invites us?" she asked as she gave Helen a slight nudge. "I haven't been here many times. I think the Old One's taken a liking to you right off." She glanced at Helen as they entered the room and then slowed to another stop. "Don't be nervous, Helen. I am quite sure he's glad you're here."

The huge, Scarlet McCaw flew from his perch, and buzzed the group so close they all ducked and watched him land in the rafters above them.

"He's looking straight at you," Helen said, glancing at Hopian.

The little Sprite smiled. "Don't mind him. He's supposed to belong to the Wizard, but I think he's his own person. If he likes you, he'll probably leave you alone. But if he doesn't… Well…you'll know it pretty quick."

Apple took to the air, flew past them, and straight up a stairway on their right.

Helen's gaze followed the parrot and to her right she could see a stone well complete with rope, crank, and bucket. "I haven't seen one of those in years," she said.

Pren laughed. "The Wizard likes to keep it basic, but Bo did put him in a freezer, stove, and refrigerator just past the well. Look in the left corner of the room. Those work benches and cabinets above and below them, are where he does his work. He has made the strangest things come from what these cabinets hold."

Pren eased from the two and walked toward the far end of the room.

"Helen…Helen!" Hopian prompted with another nudge.

"I'm still here," Helen said. "I'm just blown away with this, one room. Never seen a room like this in all of my life." She then noticed Pren, standing at the foot of the stairway with Andsell. The smile on the old Wizard's face looked genuine.

"I'm sorry," Hopian whispered. "I should have at least told you what to expect."

"Andsell! Andsell! Andsell!" The parrot screamed again as it flew down the stairway, over the two still standing at the foot, and then into the rafters above Helen and Hopian.

"Now-now, Apple," Andsell called. "We are all friends here. Go back to your perch."

Then, quick as a cat's sneeze, the huge, Scarlet McCaw sailed straight to his perch at the end of the windows and close to the work area.

Andsell stepped toward them from the base of the stairway. "The Dwarves made all this for me," he said proudly. "Borack Cliffspring ordered it himself. They watch this place as if it were L Two as well. Sharp as the Elves of Dragon's Oak they still are and twice as stubborn at what they do and how they do it."

"Come in. Come in," a young, blonde-haired girl of twenty or so said. The girl was standing on their far right, in what looked to be the kitchen. It was right across from the work benches. "I am Elisa Schmidt, John and Trudy's daughter. I've heard Grandfather Andsell speak of you many times. He thinks you are blessed with gifts you may not be aware of."

Helen smiled, picked up two sacks of supplies from the dumb waiter, and then walked toward the kitchen. The old Wizard motioned for Hopian to join him at one of the couches near the work area.

"Come, come," Elisa prompted, motioning toward Helen with the two sacks. "We'll wash and boil them right now. I hope you like them with warm butter."

"I do," Helen said, glancing back at the old Wizard as she passed. He was reclining with Hopian at the far end of the windows, quite near the door to the Dragon's walk.

As Helen sat the bags of groceries down on the table next to the sink, she could feel the old one's eyes still on her.

"Were you ever aware of what you may be?" Elisa asked as her smile widened.

"Aware…" Helen slowly turned toward the two at the couches on the far side of the great room. "Not sure of anything," Helen admitted. "When I was young, I dreamed I could levitate and fly anywhere I wanted to go." She smiled at the young girl. "But then, just when I got to enjoy it, I somehow lost the ability to dream those things I guess."

"Ever tried to really fly?" Hopian asked.

"Certainly not," Helen said. "And I'm not about to jump from that platform to test it either." She glanced at Andsell.

"Well I hope not," Andsell said with a laugh. He motioned for her to join them. "They can handle that, my dear. I have someone who wants to meet you."

Easing away from Pren and Elisa, she looked to where the old Wizard was now walking. He was headed for the door leading to the Dragon's Walk. What's more, the Dragon himself was lying just past it, watching. In front of him was Bo, a Dwarf she knew very well. Beside him was his daughter, Entwhistle. She was dressed in deerskin pants, a long, brown toga, and deerskin slippers. Entwhistle adjusted the pack on her back. Her child-like face smiled at Helen as she neared the couches close to the door. She was also holding a strange looking staff in front of her. The wood was almost white.

"Bo? Entwhistle?" Helen said weakly. As she quickly approached, the two Dwarves stepped just inside the doorway.

"My friends call me Ent," the little Dwarf said.

With proper hugs for them both, Helen stepped back smiling at the young Dwarf. "I remember you, Ent. But I haven't seen you in a while."

Entwhistle held out the staff toward the old Wizard. "This is from my father," she said, glancing back at Bo. "He said to tell you it was made of Bodock. The silver hand at the top holds a hen's egg of aquamarine, put there as you said." She glanced back at her father.

"Go on," Bo encouraged. "You're doin' just fine."

Entwhistle looked back at Helen. "My father said you would know the words."

"Indeed," Andsell said as he gently took the staff from Entwhistle. "And just what do I owe him for this beautiful piece of work?" he asked.

Ent shrugged. "He said paid in full in times past."

Bo smiled with a slight nod.

"Well I'll say," Andsell said in a soft tone. "I'll have to remember that one."

Helen looked at the old Wizard. "Your old staff, the Stick of Eefron, what happened to it?"

Andsell smiled. "Back with Eefron and still under his stone I hope," Andsell replied, looking closely at the new staff. "This one will do well I believe." He then paused, looking straight at Ent and nodded at the pack upon her back. "Stayin' with us for a time are you?"

"No Sir," the little Dwarf answered. "Got some fresh mushrooms, thyme, and wild onions for Elisa."

"Bring them quickly," Elisa said from the kitchen.

But as Ent started toward Elisa, Andsell put a gentle hand to her shoulder.

"And something else as well?" Andsell asked with a bit of a smile.

"What?" Ent froze, noticing the Old One was looking straight at her pack.

"Do not-move," Andsell said softly, but it sounded more like a warning.

As Ent's eyes gradually widened, the old Wizard lowered the new staff, pointing the head right at the pack upon her back. "Illustro," he said so loud it made everyone at the door jump.

Instantly, the green stone at the head of the staff glowed brightly, throwing shadows of those near it all over the walls around them.

Looking very uncomfortable now, Ent quickly dropped the pack and jumped back to her father.

The pack's flap moved slowly at first. Then, it started jerking about until it came loose. For a short moment, nothing happened, but then out shot a little fairy in a dark, purple dress. Almost a foot tall, she shot about the room, dodging all who were in her way, especially Apple.

"Andsell! Andsell!" The parrot screeched as it took to the air right behind the little Fae.

"It's a dark fae!" Pren exclaimed.

"Shut the door!" Phagan shouted as he pointed toward the top of the stairs with his staff.

In a flash of fog-like sparkle and hiss, Hopian's form changed into a fae of similar size as the dark one. She then shot down the long room toward the door at the top of the stairway. Seeing this, Apple gave up the chase and ended up on top of Andsell's work benches.

But, try as they did, no one could reach the stairway door before the two winged faes. Nor could they stop Hopian from tangling with the dark one.

"What now?" Helen asked as they all scrambled up the stairway toward the still open door at the top.

"Hither, thither, and yon," Andsell said, now pausing at the bottom of the staircase. Helen and the others stopped on the stairway and looked back at the old Wizard.

"Translation?" Helen asked.

Listening to the scuffle in the upstairs hallway, they all paused near the door.

"We must be careful everywhere we go and with all we deal with," Pren said as she turned to the old Wizard. "What do you know of this dark one and James Torrance?"

The old one shrugged, still listening to the struggle from the hallway, "Sounds awfully human to me. But I fear I have misjudged this one somehow. I have not seen him. Perhaps he is a dark Elf after all. The Dwarves have so named him."

"Why would you say that?" Pren asked as a crash came from upstairs. "Are there any Elves left who haven't gone back to the Sea?"

"Shouldn't we check on Hopian?" Helen asked with concern.

Phagan shrugged again with a bit of a smile. "She's a sprite. She can handle the dark one I believe." He looked at Helen. "Not that sure who went where with how many. I've been thinking on something the dragon said not long back. When he pulled that Torrance fellow off Janice Dunn and carried him to the big river, he said the man shouted something in Elfin when he was dropped into the water below."

Just then, as they were talking, someone could be heard walking down the hallway upstairs. The sound was headed toward the door they were close to.

Pren quickly stepped through the doorway and looked down the hall. "It's Hopian," she announced excitedly.

"Just me," the little Sprite said as she paused beside Pren. With mussed hair, torn blouse, and only one shoe, she looked completely out of breath. "I couldn't hold on to her and she made it to an open window in the last bedroom. I didn't think Faes were so fast. She headed straight south toward the Black Forest I think. So, I let her go." She glanced at Phagan. "Sorry. I just don't like that place. It's still doesn't feel right to me."

"That's fine, Hopian," Andsell said. He smiled at Helen. "If the dark Fae is somehow connected with Torrance, that's probably where he would be anyway, more especially if he's a Dark Elf."

"Why was she inside my pack?" Entwhistle asked.

"She was after the Bumpas staff or at least the stone?" Pren guessed.

Hopian shrugged.

"More to the point…" Pren paused, looking at Andsell. "How did she find out about it?"

"Well, matters not," Andsell grumbled as his gaze drifted back down the stairway and into the room below. "Right now, we have to find a Wizard."

Part 4
Yon Comes a Wizard—Quest for the Stone

Later that day, Helen was helping Pren after dinner. As she was sorting out the leftovers, she noticed Hopian and Andsell standing on the far side of the room. Hopian was motioning for her to come over.

"Go to him," Pren encouraged. "You need to hear what he has to say."

Laying her kitchen towel on top of the remaining dishes, Helen slowly walked toward those gathered on the far side of the room.

"How old are you, Helen?" Andsell asked.

"Sixteen Sir," she replied as she stopped at the couches near the door to the Dragon's Walk. "Is Pragamore still here?" she asked.

"Indeed," the old Wizard replied. "I think he is interested in just what I can find out about who some are calling 'Bright Helen'." He patted the couch cushion beside him as he sat down. "This shouldn't take long."

"Does this have anything to do with the Forrest Ints?" Helen asked.

"Everything, child," Andsell answered with a smile. "But mostly, in the woods of Windham and those about it, you will now be watched by another."

Helen slowly sat up on the front edge of the couch. "Who will this be?" she managed.

Andsell slowly looked at her over his half-moon, gold, wire-rimmed glasses. "I'll only say you already know and trust him. He'll come to you in his own, good time. That is, if you take the path least trodden."

"The one of a White Witch?" Helen guessed; her tone troubled.

"That is true, young Magus. But only if you choose to do so," Andsell said. "You must say aloud your intentions my dear. That will make it an oath of sorts."

"Oh boy! Here we go!" Hopian shouted. The little Sprite jumped to her feet from the nearest couch, ran to the platform door, and then flung it open, causing Pragamore to struggle to his feet. "It's happening! It's happening!" she exclaimed.

Hearing the dragon roar his approval, Pren laughed at the little Sprite's excitement. She then turned to look at Helen. "The forest faes are here! They will hardly come inside the houses of men, but this might be an exception."

"Oh goodness," Andsell grumbled. "This will take all day."

All of a sudden, two Faes shot passed the dragon, blew passed Hopian, and then streaked up into the rafters above those at the couches.

Hopian watched them as best she could. "It's Rosebud and Lilly Ann. Woodland Faes from Kiendom are here!" she announced excitedly.

Helen quickly stood and looked toward the two Faes on the rafters above them, but all she got was wide-eyed smiles; not a single word from them at all.

Andsell looked at Helen. "Go and stand by the door with Hopian." The old Wizard struggled to his feet and looked at the little Sprite at the doorway. "The Staff of Bumpus if you please," he said in a soft tone.

Wasting no time, Hopian ran from the door, jumped upon the couch under the staff rack, and grabbed the staff from where Andsell had just put it.

"Tut-tut-tut," the old Wizard said, stopping her still atop the couch's cushion. "Place its foot upon the floor and then release it," he added.

"What?" Hopian squinted with, "Right here?"

"Right where you stand," Andsell said.

Still a bit confused, the little Sprite held out the staff of Bumpus, placed its foot on the floor, then released it.

"Well bless me," Hopian said, staring at the staff seemingly standing on its own.

"Now…" Andsell handed Helen a small piece of paper. "Read aloud the two words I have just given you."

Helen looked down at the paper then back up at the staff. "Kom Toppae," she said softly.

The six-foot limb of bodock shot across the room toward the young girl. "What?" Helen fell back against the open door and raised her arms about her head. But, not feeling a thing, and hearing only laughter from uncountable faes now sitting around Lilly Ann and Rosebud, Helen slowly opened her eyes to see the Staff of Bumpus standing only a short reach in front of her.

"Tut-tut-tut!" the old Wizard scolded, causing all to become quiet. "Remain quiet!" he shouted. He then looked at Helen. "Take your staff," he commanded. "You called it did you not?"

"I…I…did?" Helen stammered. But as she took hold of the staff, it refused to move. Quickly removing her hand, she looked puzzled at Andsell.

The old Wizard's smile widened. "Kom Toppae simply means 'Come to me'," he explained softly.

"But…" Helen squinted at Andsell. "It won't move."

"You must say the words," Hopian said. "I will seek to do good, forever fight evil, and strive to be a beacon of hope for the downtrodden."

Andsell nodded with a smile. "Repeat that," he said softly.

Helen nodded. "I will seek to do good, forever fight evil, and strive to be a beacon of hope for the downtrodden," she repeated.

"Now, the Staff of Bumpus is yours for the taking," Andsell said.

Pausing for a moment, Helen looked about the room. Everyone there, Faes and Human folk alike, seemed to be holding their breath.

"Take it!" Hopian prompted as she moved up beside Helen.

With that, Helen slowly reached for the still standing limb of Bodock. As her hand neared the staff, a bright blue bolt of energy shot from it and into her hand, followed by the staff itself. Holding tightly to it, Helen gasped then stumbled backwards.

"Got-cha," Hopian said loudly. The little Sprite grabbed Helen's right arm and lowered her gently to her knees.

"Jeez!" Helen exclaimed, still gripping the staff of Bumpus.

The huge room immediately filled with sound—cheering, shouting, and clapping alike.

Helen slowly looked up into the rafters, which now seemed to be filled with even more Faes. "Where did they come from? There are too many to count," she asked.

"Matters not," the old Wizard said with a bit of a smile. "You were supposed to take the staff, Helen. After all you called it. Always remember, *Kom Toppae* means 'come to me'. Now, can you stand?"

Helen slowly stood, with Hopian still gripping her right arm tightly. Leaning heavily on the staff, she looked at Andsell. "Would have been nice to know," she grumbled. What in the shocking blue-eyed wonder just hit me?

"Oh…" Andsell smiled sheepishly. "That was me. I gave you a present," the old Wizard admitted. "From time to time, you will remember things you will realize you had no way of knowing. Now, at least you will know where they all came from." His smile widened as he continued to look at the young girl. "Now, are we off or on?"

"Sir?" she asked puzzled.

Hopian leaned closer to Helen and whispered, "You'll have to agree to this in your own words, My Lady. If not, you'll never be a White Witch."

"White Witch?" Helen asked weakly.

"A female Wizard," Andsell said. "You'll live right here with us. That is, if you choose to."

Helen's smile widened as she looked at the pale, green stone upon the head of the staff. "Then, I choose that path," she said, staring back at Andsell. "I am on!" she added loudly.

Again, the cheers went up, but this time the Faes all took to the air, sending Hopian scrambling toward the still open door of Dragon's Walk. The excited roar of the Dragon only added to the excitement as the little ones scrambled to leave the 'man's cave'.

"Wonderful!" Pren said as she ran to Helen and gave her a proper hug.

"You'll live right here with us and train under Andsell," Elisa added, also looking very excited.

"Here?" Helen's gaze froze on the old Wizard. His smile seemed as bright as his eyes.

"I am one hundred and ninety-eight years old, young one," he explained. "My strength is not as it was when I was half that. I have two years before the Elves come for me. I desperately need an apprentice to fill my shoes and service the area graced to me by the White just before he himself left with the Elves as well. The world of men is now fully upon us and we are, so to say, losing our influence in it. Whitestone Castle is no more and the Wizard Richard Alvis is gone with it. Soon, the spell he cast, that now protects us from the eyes of men, will fade. You are our only hope to continue that."

Helen paused, her eyes locked on Andsell. "Is that why the Ints have been protecting me? Was it a truth I was not privy to know just then? They were protecting what you were hoping I would become …a White Witch?"

Pren gently stroked her back. "Does that scare you, My Lady?"

"Only when I said 'Yes'," Helen said weakly. She gradually looked back at the old Wizard. "I have given it a great deal of thought and had already come to the conclusion that in no way could I say 'no'."

"We applaud your decision, My Lady," Andsell said as he stepped within a short distance of Helen. "This is not an easy life, but it's one you can be proud of, young Magus. The final question is will you become my apprentice?"

Helen took a half step backwards as her mouth slowly opened. "I would like that, but I thought I already was," she managed weakly.

"That's a 'YES'! Rosebud and Lilly Ann shouted in unison as they cheered and flew about the rafters.

"They didn't leave?" Helen asked.

"Tut-tut-tut!" Andsell said, quieting the little ones instantly. "Of course they didn't leave. They will be your 'watch' as they always have for me. Remember that." He stretched out his hand toward the staff. "*Kom Toppae*," he said softly.

Instantly the staff pulled away from Helen and went to the hand now reaching for it.

"You have passed the three tests, young Helen," he said softly. "The Staff of Bumpus was the third test. The first was hearing the Ints in the trees and you did well with that. The second was when you stood up to the Witch Ibenus, and a Black Witch she was as well. But…" He paused and winked at her. "We have just planted the acorn. Now, we can water it and watch as it sprouts into a great, white oak."

Andsell's gaze drifted toward the huge windows in front of the Rift. Helen watched him closely, for it seemed his thoughts went out much farther than that.

Looking back at his granddaughter, he finally said, "We still have a little time for the map and your supplies."

"Got 'em," Pren said. She turned and trotted toward the kitchen at the far end of the great room.

"Map? Supplies?" Helen asked weakly.

Helen looked back toward the kitchen. Elisa was now with Pren, both now darting here and there about the kitchen and stuffing various things into two, large satchels. The young White slowly stood, looking closely at the satchels. They were joined at their tops by heavy leather straps. She looked back at the old Wizard.

"Map! Map! Map!" Pren grumbled, still looking about the kitchen.

"What map?" Helen asked.

Andsell shrugged as he sat down in a large, padded chair next to one of the huge windows. "The map she is hopefully trying to find will show you the way to a place I hope still exists. At least be there the way it used to be. Back in the day, it was called The Hollow Mountains by those who knew it way back then. But, all in all, that piece of parchment is just for you. Your 'way' to that area is still standing on the Dragon's Walk. He's eagerly though patiently waiting to take you to a place of his past."

"The Hollow Mountains?" Helen's blank stare slowly made its way to the windows, escaping for just a moment. "Isn't that where the old Wizard of Whitestone got his dragon?"

"Actually his first dragon," Andsell said. "That would be Richard Alvis at the Crystal Lake I believe. That lake is actually inside the huge cavern you will be hopefully visiting."

"But…but that was several hundred years ago," Helen said. "Bo spoke of him many times."

"True as well," Andsell replied.

"But…but, what am I to do there?" a well confused Helen asked.

Andsell slowly reached atop the staff in his left hand, removed the blue-green stone from the silver hand at its head, and put it in his pocket. He handed the staff of Bumpus back to Helen "That stone is mine, My Lady. You will have to find your own within that very cavern. Speak to the Lady of the Lake. She will help you with that I am sure."

"Lady of the Lake?" Helen's squint deepened. "Did the Wizard Richard do that?" she asked curiously.

Andsell scratched the back of his head. "Not as I recall. He was looking for a dragon way back then. Not sure there are any left after all this time has passed. They may have been taken with the Elves as well."

"But…but what if that place is no longer there? What if there are dragons still there?" Helen's question brought a frown from the old Wizard.

"No more 'what ifs'," he grumbled. "Would I send you if I didn't think it so? The Dragon will know and make the proper decision at that time. Give that the respect it deserves. We're just going through the proper motions right now young Helen. Every Wizard from times past had to go to the Hollow Mountains in search of himself, or herself as the case might have been." He glared at Helen. "Are you still my student? Are you off or on?" he demanded.

"Sorry Sir," Helen mumbled, looking embarrassed. "I am on, Sir. What must I do? Didn't the Wizard Richard walk his way to the Hollow Mountains?"

"He did indeed," Andsell said. "But that was for a particular purpose—to bring clarity to himself. Your 'walk', Bright Helen, stands before you. It is me. As for your 'way', he is still waiting for you on the Dragon's Walk. This is twenty-twenty three. No one believes in Dragons anymore, let alone Wizards. You will leave just after sunset this evening. We'll take care of the packing and all. It's now just after two PM. Go upstairs and try to get some rest for the journey. I'll send Pren to your grandparents and tell them what has happened and where you will be. They will need to know as well. They can inform your father in London if need be." He paused, studying Helen's blank expression. "I know this is a great task to put upon such a young apprentice, but I believe you are up to the challenge."

Helen gradually backed from the old Wizard, but kept eye contact with him. "Please have someone wake me when it's time to leave," she said. "I will continue on this journey and do the best I can."

The smile on Andsell's face could hardly be matched as he watched her slowly walk up the stairway toward the bedrooms.

Hopian ease up beside the old Wizard. "Will she be all right? She looks full of doubt," she whispered.

"Of course she is," whispered Andsell. "Doubt is but the fog that hides the truth. The dragon will clear the way for her I am sure."

~ * ~

With the bedroom's huge oak door closed and its heavy drapes pulled, the room upstairs had become totally dark. Not even the sound of a cricket could be heard. With quilt and spread pushed to the foot, Helen lay between the clean sheets Pren had provided. But with the events of the day constantly replaying through her head, she could find no calm spot at all. The 'what ifs' kept her mind spinning as did the long ride with Pragamore to a place she had only heard Bo speak of in countless stories of the past. Finally, thinking of who the Lady of the Lake could be, her eyes slowly closed.

~ * ~

"Helen…Helen," a soft voice said from the darkness.

Slowly opening her eyes, Helen could see a light coming through her partially open bedroom door.

"Pereen?" she managed. "You are here? Where is Pren?"

"She is still here as well," the White answered as she eased inside. "I was told you are now training under Andsell and he was sending you to the Hollow Mountains."

Pereen sat down on the edge of the bed and brushed her long, brown hair back behind her shoulders. She watched Helen as she sat up on the edge with her.

"I have committed to that," Helen said. "Is it time to go?"

"Almost." Pereen turned on the table lamp. She then nodded toward a straight-back chair beside the door. "We're about the same size. The jeans are a bit stiff, but you'll need them in the brisk wind. There's a hooded, rainproof coat there as well as a heavy shirt." She handed Helen a large, plastic bag full of something cut into one-inch squares. Fairly soft they were, colored with a strange, wine-like hue.

"Pemmican," Pereen said. "They are ground beef jerky with raisins and walnuts. Pragamore has already been fed. This will be a long trip for him, Helen. He is well up in his years but wants very much to make it. If he seems weak and winded, insist he put down somewhere safe and rest, well away from prying eyes. You should make it in about four to five hours or so, depending on how many times you have to put down. Do not let the dawn catch you two in the air. Hide somewhere until dusk comes again. Understand?"

Helen nodded. "I'll be downstairs in a minute or so," she added.

~ * ~

Ten minutes later, somewhere close to 8:00PM, Helen eased down the stairway toward the great room. Looking toward the far end of the room, she could see the old Wizard, sitting with Pereen, Pren, Elisa, and Hopian as well. The Dragon seemed to be resting on the Walk fairly close to the door. He was being tended by Bo, Broderick, and several more Dwarves.

Helen paused at the foot of the stairs, holding her rainproof coat in her arms. "Are they all from Leachenwood?" she asked.

"Oh…" Andsell quickly struggled to his feet. "And L Two as well," he answered. He motioned for her to come and join them. "They are putting the final touches on the saddle." He pointed to a particularly heavy-set, red-haired Dwarf who was checking the tethers. He looked like a hunter in his red plaid shirt and faded Levis. "He's called Gremniss Meechum, My Lady. He is one of the leaders here at the Rift and is in the Queen's line. Looks after Pragamore as well." He chuckled, still looking at Helen. "He actually works at a sporting goods place as a gunsmith. Now-a-days, outsiders don't know the difference between Dwarves and midgets."

"Walk softly around him, Helen," Pereen advised. "He's stubborn and not that keen on Pragamore making the trip. But, since the Dragon insisted, he has reluctantly given a little ground."

"Well, com'mon if yer commin'," shouted the very one they were speaking of.

Helen eyed the heavy-set Dwarf as she and the others stepped out onto the platform. His eyes looked kind, but sorely troubled none-the-less.

"Last one of 'em ya know," Gremniss grumbled, staring at Helen. "That's a great, long stretch you're fixin' ta start on Lass. It's one he hasn't flown in a great number of years."

"Yes, Sir," Helen said. "I'm—"

"I know who you are, Lass," the Dwarf grumbled. "You can call me Lloyd." He looked at Pereen.

"She is aware of all of that," Pereen said. "We've planned all of this out."

"Planned it did ya say?" The frown deepened on the Dwarf's face. "I don't think—"

Pragamore blew a hot torrent from his nose, sending the Dwarf's hat tumbling from the edge of the platform. "Enough!" the dragon exclaimed. "This is NOT your decision, Master Dwarf. Neither is it young Helen's. IT! IS! MINE! Before I die, I would, one last time, like to watch a wizard work within the Cave of Mirrors. Is that too much to ask?"

"But…" Gremniss reached to his head for a hat that was no

longer there. Failing to find it, he edged closer to the Dragon. "You are tha last of your kind. You're tha last Great Winged Forest Dragon any of us will ever know of. There simply is not one other. All of us Dwarves here have made it our duty to protect and take care of ya. If ya leave here, we simply cannot do that in any way I know of."

"I understand and appreciate that," Pragamore said. "But I serve Bright Helen now. The days of Richard of Whitestone are long gone, and I am privileged to have yet another Wizard. You should worry about me if I refuse to go, Master Dwarf, not in my going." His huge head slowly turned to Pareen. "Are you ready, My Lady?" he asked.

"We are," Pereen answered, slightly smiling at Helen.

Helen instantly wheeled toward the young White. "Are you going with me?" she asked excitedly.

Pareen's smile widened with a nod. "Grimness convinced Andsell to this one exception. You wouldn't mind a little company, would you?"

Helen took a deep breath. "Absolutely not," she said. "Actually, I am quite relieved to have a little company." She quickly smiled at the Dragon. "No offense of course."

"None take, My Lady," Pragamore said. "Two White's on the trip? What could be safer?"

~ * ~

Thirty minutes later, sitting in the forward seat of the dragon's saddle, Helen looked all around her as the dragon silently glided just above the white clouds. Many of them looked like snow on the fields of home, but she knew that illusion was not so. The night sky was exactly opposite. It looked as if many diamonds were sprinkled upon a blanket of dark, purple velvet. Taking unmeasurable comfort in the knowledge Pereen was with her, the young White, finally, was able to relax. The unmatched view from the front seat took Helen's breath at times—the slow, rowing motion of the Dragon's wings, the view of the land below as the clouds parted at times, and the wondrous thought that there must be someone higher in the world that controlled everything, even the Wizards. Hours passed without incident or much conversation. If one talked, it was a must to almost shout to get above the sound of the wind. Then, well into what Helen thought must be the third hour, the rowing motion stopped.

For the first time, the old Dragon changed direction, banking slightly to his right.

Helen leaned slightly back and turned to Pereen. "What's happening?" she asked loudly. "Why did we change direction? Is everything all right?"

"I believe so," Pereen answered. "Look below. See that large, darkened spot with a bright light in its middle?"

Leaning slightly to her left, Helen nodded. "Why are we circling it?"

"That is a beacon Andsell had set at Connell Gordin's Safe Haven Ranch. She is a half-elf and has an unmatched love for animals, especially Dragons. The Elves of Dragon's Oak bought it for her many years ago. Much like they did the Hollow Mountains— a total of five hundred acres or more in that deal. Andsell has set up a stop for Pragamore with Connell. We'll be—"

The old Dragon dropped suddenly, causing the girls to grab for the saddle bars. He then went into a slow, downward spiral.

"Jeez," Helen gasped as her hair flew wildly in the wind. "She looked back at Pereen again. "You mean you've already been here?"

Pereen smiled with a nod. "But not at all to the Hollow Mountains, let alone the Crystal Cave. Not many are allowed there these days. Even old Phagan was unaware of the changes. The world of men is not—"

"Whoa!" they both cried as Pragamore dipped sharply, and they both grabbed the bars.

"He's heading there," Pereen said as she pointed out the huge, bright bonfire just below them. With flames thirty feet tall and at least twelve feet at its base, it cast a beacon that could be seen for miles.

Pragamore glanced back at Helen. "We are here, My Lady," he said.

"You sound winded, old friend," Pereen said. "Are you feeling well?"

"Not exactly what I used to be," the Dragon answered. "We will be put back a day I'm afraid. Does that disappoint you?"

Pren smiled. "Not in the least. You are a blessing to us all, Pragamore. Nothing you do disappoints us."

Then, as the great Dragon glided closer to the ground, both Helen and Pereen could clearly hear the cheering of those gathered across the grassy field in front of them. Three dozen or more, they stood near the fire and looked to be a mixture of Dwarf, Elfin, and Men alike.

Pereen leaned forward and patted the Dragon's right side. "Do you see the barn, Pragamore?" she shouted.

"I do, My Lady," the Dragon answered.

"Good," Pereen shouted. "Come in over the gathering at the bonfire and land close to the barn doors."

"After you get off, may I then go into the barn?" Pragamore asked.

"You may," Pereen said. "But, there are two or three who will want to see you. After all, you are still known to them as the Dragon of the old Wizard Richard Alvis. They will, no doubt, have many questions."

"Is Connell one of them?" Pragamore asked.

"I believe she will be," Pereen answered. "She is married to—"

"Night Wing," the Dragon interrupted, sounding a bit excited. "I remember the huge raven, Soot, quite vividly. His given name is Master Glain. He was cursed by the evil Wizard named Nimbsfork I believe. Did Connell cure him of that or does he still fly at times?"

"To a point," Pereen said. "But he still flies at night I am told."

With those words, the Dragon set a straight and steady course, descending over the field, those at the beacon fire, and on toward the barn. Hitting the ground at a slight run, the three ended up just a weak, stone's throw from the barn's huge, front doors.

"Hold!" a man shouted somewhere behind them.

Helen quickly turned to see a man trying to hold back the crowd. Clearly over six feet tall and with an impressive build, he was still having trouble with their excitement.

"Get off quick," Pereen said as they fumbled with their tethers. "Let's get Pragamore into the barn and close the doors."

Quickly working toward that, Pereen looked at the Dragon. "Take the first stall. It should be clean and ready." Pereen gathered her collar close about her neck. "Never knew April could be so cold," she grumbled.

In less than a minute, the Dragon was inside and out of sight, leaving the two ladies standing just outside the partially open doors.

"Hold!" came the shout again, almost angry sounding this time.

Helen and Pereen looked to see the same man still trying to

slow the slowly advancing crowd.

"A Dragon does not fellowship with a stranger, let alone a mob of them!" the man shouted angrily.

Now, the tall man was joined by a lady of long, sandy blonde hair, those trying to get near the barn stopped immediately.

"We only want to see the Dragon," one from the crowd said. "After all, this may be our last chance. Please."

"I understand," the lady said. "But you must choose one to speak for you. We will then go and welcome our guests. All the rest will stay right here or must I call the archers."

Quickly talking among themselves, a little man finally stepped from the group.

"Plead our request, Master Keating," several from the crowd said.

"Thank you! Thank you!" He bowed slightly to the crowd as he joined the tall man and the blonde woman.

Back at the barn, the two girls watched intently.

"That's Connell and Glain Cerrig," Pereen whispered.

"Who is with them?" Pragamore asked, now easing up from the shadows of the barn.

"Not at all sure," Pereen said. "They called him Master Keating. He looks like an old Elf I believe and about five and a half feet tall. His hair is thin and white, his eyebrows a bit bushy, and he walks with a cane. But I can't see his ears."

Pereen took a step forward. "Connell! Glain! Who do you have with you?"

"The Elf, Master Byron Keating," Connell said.

Connell then slowed to a stop a few paces from Pereen and looked passed her and Helen. But the Dragon had returned, once again, to the barn's shadows.

Now, with mouth slightly agape, Connell eased passed Byron and on toward Helen and Pereen at the barn door. But, not to be outdone, Master Keating stayed right behind her. As they neared Helen and Pereen, they both stopped, staring into the darkness of the barn's great room.

Master Keating stepped slightly forward, still captivated by the darkness of the barn. "Pragamore? I know your name. Do you not remember your old friend, Byron Keating? Do you not remember the friend of your Wizard, Richard Alvis?"

"I do," came the deep, guttural response from the darkness of the barn. "You are still alive?"

"I am indeed." Bryon eased past the ladies. Leaning heavily on his cane, he edged closer to the open doors. But the brightness of the fire behind him only hid the features of the silhouette he was now trying to make sense of. "You are an anomaly, old friend— something we expected to NEVER see again."

"Never is a long, long time, Bryon Keating," the voice from the darkness said.

"It is truly that," Bryon agreed. "I truly feel as if I have lived forever at times. We are told by the Wizard Andsell, the Dwarves of Leachenwood have protected you all of these, long years."

"They did that," the Dragon said. "But that would be the Dwarves of L Two and Phagan's Rift as it were."

"Leachenwood Two," the Elf repeated softly as he nodded. "I, myself, look back to Dragon's Oak and the Elves of Show Lake."

"Those places only exist in our memories these days," the Dragon replied. "They have moved from us to Valinor in the sea."

"True as well," Byron agreed. "This world of men is still blessed with but a few of us from those days, old friend."

"And we are still blessed to be a part of it," Connell said as she and Glain stepped up beside the old Dwarf. "May we still look upon you as friends, Pragamore?"

Then, ever so slowly, the darkened shadows gave way to shape and color as the Great-Winged Dragon stepped back into the light.

Connell's smile widened. "Emerald green and yellow breast was never more beautiful," she said. Tears streamed down her face as she looked into the Dragon's huge, yellow eyes. "You are as beautiful as I have always remembered the others."

Stepping a little closer, Pragamore looked down at Connell. "Didn't mean to make you sad, My Lady," he said softly. His mulish ears swung forward.

"You didn't," Connell said. "Tears of joy, really. I am now recalling the others of your kind."

"That would be Pandahar, Kraiton, Ravenclaw and the Oxbow—"

"Beautraux!" Glain said, smiling at the Dragon.

Pragamore paused to look at the one who had just spoken. "Tell me, Glain Cerrig, do you still see much of Soot now-a-days or has

Connell washed that Nimbsfork poison from you?"

Glain smiled, glancing at Pren and Helen. "Somewhat," he admitted. "But I have learned to cope with what is left me."

Bryon, leaning heavily on his cane, slowly stepped closer to the Dragon, causing Pragamore to lift his head slightly. "We are told you are to go to the Hollow Mountains and train with a Wizard to replace Andsell. Yet, you have brought only two young women with you."

"That is true, Master Keating," the Dragon said. "The younger is Helen Durkin, a young White. Still in the Wizard's care she is. But the older of them is Pereen Willingham, a White Witch of experience."

At those words, a hush fell upon all those still near the fire for the words and actions of a Wizard were still revered by all there.

"Now what?" Pereen whispered to Helen.

"Have not a clue," Helen replied.

"We eat and celebrate!" Glain said loudly. He looked at the Dragon. "We have a fresh deer just killed. Would that please you?"

"It would, and water if possible," the Dragon said.

Glain quickly looked toward those at the fire. "Send two to fetch the deer and two more for water for our Dragon. We will have guests this night!" he added loudly.

Immediately, four broke from those at the fire and ran for the pump.

Glain looked back at Helen. "I know you," he started. "You are the grandchild of the Watcher in the Woods, old Professor Robert Durkin, are you not? Bo has spoken many kind words about you." He looked at Pereen. "And she is…"

"Pereen Willingham, our White," Helen said. "She is making the journey with us to keep me grounded."

Pereen smiled at the young man, for his expression was more than kind. "We go to the Hollow Mountains to raise a stone for Helen's staff. We are told the place is still there."

"It is that," Glain responded, still holding his smile. "My Lady, The Valley remains much like it was in the past, save a few alterations put there by the Dwarves and Elves alike; as is the Cave of Mirrors."

"Valley?" Helen stared at the older man. "I thought it was in the mountains."

That remark brought a solid round of laughter from those still at the bonfire.

Glain, laughing as well, added, "The mountains are indeed close about. They border the east side of the valley. That description, Hollow Mountains, was just a play on words by the Old Ones of the time in order to confuse any outsiders. Some, back then, were inclined to refer to a valley as a 'hollow' as it were. Your journey thus far has taken you about two thirds of the way to that very place. You are now just south of Gossimer Swamp." He turned to the Dragon. "These young ones have little knowledge of where they are or where they are going, Pragamore. I trust you still remember the way, my old friend."

"Like my father before me," the Dragon replied. "Bear southwest of here, past the Cuttoff Lake, and Dragon's Oak to the west. I should then have the Crystal Lake in sight if I am high enough. Keeping the mountain line on my left, I should soon see a long, green valley. The Cave of Mirrors is at the southern end of that valley."

Glain laughed loudly and clapped his hands. "Good enough, old friend. He glanced at Helen. "That was called the Valley of the Unicorns by those back then. The Whitestone Road ends right there by the way. Now…" He paused, looking at Pereen and Helen again. "The hog is still on the fire, but it should be about ready for us. They are still basting it with spices and brown sugar. We have fresh rolls, baked sweet potatoes, and a huge pot of lima beans and ham. Won't you join us?"

"Thank you. We would love to," Pereen said.

~ * ~

That night, and well into the early morning hours, was good rest for Pereen, Helen, and the Dragon. About 7:00AM the next day, a noise woke Helen. It was one she wasn't familiar with. Swinging her feet to the cold, wooden floor, she ran to the nearest window and looked outside.

"They have a plane here," she said as she watched a medium-sized, yellow, twin-engine plane taxi out on the flat field of a runway.

Dressing quickly, she stepped into the hallway and met Pereen evidently doing the same thing.

"An aero plane just took off from here," Helen said.

Byron, walked up and joined them. "That would be Glain and

Connell," he said. "They are going ahead of you and make sure the beacon fires are lit in proper time. Glain was impressed by how much the Dragon remembered, but the Wizard Phagan insisted on the fires anyways."

Byron smiled. "For now, let us go to the dining area and check out the cook's smorgasbord."

"Oh boy," Helen replied. "That sounds fantastic."

"It is," Byron said. "The cook didn't know what you two would like, so he made a little of everything. It's the best breakfast ever—eggs, bacon, sausage, fried potatoes smothered in onions, and cheesy grits. There's hot cakes if you have a mind for the sweet. The hunters have even killed another deer for the Dragon. He should be getting it as we eat as well."

Part 5
Surprise at the Cave of Mirrors

Late that evening, everyone at Safe Haven gathered close to the front of the barn to watch Connell and Helen saddle the Dragon. Remaining strangely quiet, almost subdued, Pragamore ignored those gathered only fifty feet from him. Helen noticed his gaze held straight south, seemingly looking at something only he could see…

"Don't be nervous about our on-lookers, Pragamore," Connell said. "They all but begged to see you today and I allowed it. I hope it is well with you."

The Dragon slowly turned toward her. "It is, My Lady," the Dragon said. "It does not trouble me. I am concerned about other things right now," he added as he looked toward the south once more.

"Pragamore?" Connell watched his expression closely.

But she didn't get answer, as the Dragon appeared to be in deep thought. Connell eased closer to the Dragon's head and looked in the same direction that held his attention. Then, she saw it. It was only a flash of yellowish green at first, but it came again and again as it moved through the trees in the distance. It seemed to drift with the breeze at times, and then against it at others.

"That's strange," Helen said, observing the flashes as well.

Although her voice was not much more than a whisper, it made Connell jump and look back at her. "Do you see that?" she asked quietly.

"Don't know what I saw," Helen admitted. "Pale green with a touch of yellow at times."

They both then turned to the Dragon as if for answers.

"Not that sure myself," Pragamore admitted. "But what or whoever it was knows we are here. It was much closer at first, but when I started watching, it slowly moved away from us." He paused, looking toward the south again. "It called to me. I am sure of it. 'This way,' she said and called me by name as well."

"She?" Helen asked. "It was a she?"

The Dragon slowly nodded and looked down at the saddle lying before him in the grass. "It was not a man, but the voice of a young girl I heard." He glanced back at Pereen. "It's getting dark." He nodded at the saddle. "Put this thing on me and we'll fly and perhaps solve this riddle along the way."

~ * ~

Keeping the Green River on his left, the great Dragon climbed, but didn't reach the altitude he attained on the first leg of their journey. Then, as the full moon shone, Pereen, now in the front saddle, got a very quick glimpse of something that passed in front of them and sped off, bearing more to the west. "This way," came the voice on the wind. Try as she did, she could not follow, for it proved much too fast.

"I saw it as well," Pragamore said. He dropped his right wing slightly and continued more westward.

Helen, leaned forward and tapped on Pereen's shoulder. "I saw the orb also. We're following it more to the west?"

Pereen nodded. "Pragamore is now heading toward Dragon's Oak, the old home of the White Elves I think. The orb left us in that, same direction. I somehow believe he knows what it is, or he wouldn't be following it so freely."

After passing over a small forest, Helen noticed the moon's glint on the river had gone. Instead, she saw the beginning of a large range of mountains to her left.

"Pereen! Pereen!" she said excitedly. "Are those the Hollow Mountains?"

Pereen looked back and nodded. "Yes. We are over the valley past Wizards have referred to as a 'Hollow'. This is the last leg of—"

Before she could say another word, Pragamore shuddered and dipped sharply.

Grabbing for the saddle bar, Pereen shouted, "Pragamore, what was that?"

"Not sure," the Dragon said. "I've been having dizzy spells lately and blurred vision as well. They come and go quickly and only leave me guessing.

"And there is another beacon in the field," Pereen said.

Dipping even lower, Pragamore went into a slow glide straight toward the bonfire. Slowly carrying them across grassy meadows, small patches of woods, and weedy fields, he continued toward the soft glow of the beacon. Over a vast and level field of grass he finally glided, getting so low it seemed only a jump to the ground. Then, just as Pereen was about to ask the obvious question, she noticed several buildings on a flat outcropping on their left. It was low enough to be accessed from a wide stair extending from the top to the field below. The Dragon's head rose sharply as his wings caught the air. The sudden slow, again, causing Helen and Pereen to grab their saddle bars.

The Dragon landed softly, just a short walk from the stairway leading up the side of the outcropping. Helen stood in the stirrups. "There's that yellow plane again!" she exclaimed. "Connell and Glain are already here."

The great Dragon knelt to the grass for the ladies to dismount as a round of cheers went up from a little group awaiting their arrival. Both men and women, some with children, ran the short distance to them. They all but encircled the Dragon and ladies, keeping their distance from the great creature.

Lowering his head close to Pereen, Pragamore whispered, "Is there not a barn close?"

"I don't think so," Pereen said, seeing more than two dozen people watching them. She leaned against Pragamore's neck. "Just remember these are your friends. Some of whom have never seen a Dragon, let alone spoke to one. But, through countless stories and fairy tales, they know well of you none-the-less."

Helen eased up beside Pereen and looked at Pragamore, but didn't say anything.

"My Lady?" the Dragon asked, seeing she was watching him intently.

Helen smiled at the Dragon. "Speaking of friends, it has become quite obvious you have solved the riddle of the glowing orb. You know who it was or you would not have followed it as you did."

"Hopian," the Dragon said. "I remembered the tone of her voice. Besides, she's the only something I know who can move in a point of light."

As he was speaking, two, young men dressed like woodsmen, approached. Each carrying two wooden buckets of what looked to be water.

"Oh, good," the Dragon whispered. "They have water for me."

Stopping a few paces from the three, one of them looked at

Pereen. "Would the Dragon Pragamore like some water?" he asked.

"He would," Pragamore said.

The two, now with mouths agape, slowly turned toward the Dragon.

Moving more in front of him, one of them said, "As I live and breathe, the stories I have heard since a child must all true?"

"Depends upon just what you have heard," the Dragon said, now a bit amused.

"Come," the other man said, and they lifted their buckets and walked closer. Sitting their buckets in front of the Dragon, he added, "We have food if you are hungry."

"Are you hungry?" Pereen asked.

"No, My Lady," Pragamore replied. "Is the Cave of Mirrors near?" he asked the men.

"Quite near," one answered. "Just walk the path before you. It will lead you up that stairway and between two buildings. From there, that part of the path is lined with touches. You can see the entrance from there. We will go with you if it pleases you."

"It does," the Dragon said as he looked at the ladies. "I will wait for you inside the cave."

"Do you feel all right?" Helen asked.

"Yes, My Lady," the Dragon said. "I'm just a little winded, I think. After I drink, I will rest beside the lake."

But the Dragon didn't move. Instead, his eyes remained on the foot of the stairway. The crowd that had circled them, had moved and were now gathered on the walkway at the foot of the stairs, all but blocking it.

Helen looked toward those at the stairs. "Please make way for him to pass," she called.

Now, seeing them move to one side or the other, Pragamore proceeded toward the stairway. As he started between them, he closed his eyes but kept walking with the girls and those who provided the water right behind him. Many of the Dwarves, Elves, and Men alike politely gave ground and moved back. But some of the brave souls eased forward, letting their hands gently brush the Dragon's sides.

"Do not touch the Dragon," Glain said as he and Connell waited for the little group at the top of the wide stairway.

"Please, do not scold them," Connell said. "Some believe to touch a Dragon is to bring good luck."

"Do not fear them, Pragamore," one of the men who brought the water said. "They only want to touch what they have tried so hard to believe in all these many years."

Pereen and Helen paused with Connell and Glain at the top of the stairway.

"The trip was hard on him," Pereen said to Connell. "Should we let him return by himself?"

Glain smiled. "That's one reason we brought the Beechcraft. Besides, the Dwarves have provided three bushels of sweet potatoes for him. We must carry those back as well. Come, let us continue. We want to see how you get that stone."

Helen shrugged as they walked behind Pragamore. "Just go to the point and call her name," she explained.

"Point?" Connell asked. "Where is that and what name?"

Helen shrugged again as the little group made their way between the two buildings. "Grandfather said I would know where to go once I get there. He said her name is Andrea Amora, the Lady of the Lake at the Valley of the Unicorns."

That brought only raised eyebrows from both Glain as well as Connell.

Once past the buildings, two Elfin guards stepped forward and stopped those who were following close behind them. "The Wizard Phagan has told us of these," one called to the group now watching closely. "They are to be allowed access and no others."

Now, at the head of a much shorter path, paved with flat field stones, Helen looked toward the gaping mouth of a place she had only heard Bo mention in his many stories.

Two other guards immediately rushed from the little group and started lighting torches along the walls of the cave as Pereen and Helen slowly walked forward. But not until they both noticed Pragamore did they enter. The Dragon was on the left side of what looked like a forty-foot-wide stone floor. With a wall of rock on its left side, it was bordered by a huge, crystal blue lake on its right. Being a bit chilly, the guards seemed to be busying themselves by making a small fire for the Dragon.

"This place is carved out of the mountain," Helen said as she stepped onto the smooth, stone floor. The lake, on her right, reached as far as she could see, seemingly right under the huge mountain. At its near bank a small jetty extended out into the water. Almost paralleling the wall on their right at times, it then reached forty paces or more out into the lake.

"There it is." Pereen nudged Helen. "There is your point. The start of it is only a weak stone's throw from us."

Helen eased forward, but stopped, glancing back at the little group.

"Don't falter now," Pereen said. "Andsell has set your feet upon this path. You must now go and collect what he wants you to have."

Easing forward without another word, Helen stepped upon the twenty-foot wide jetty. It looked to be a warning to her, for it pointed straight toward the darkness which hid well the far side of the lake. But there was only one torch burning upon the near wall of the cavern behind Helen. To her, it projected her shadow—an uneasy figure of a girl upon the water.

"Go!" Connell said encouraging her. "This is something the Old One said you must do alone. We will remain at the mouth of the cave."

Even though Helen found no comfort in that at all, she continued. With clinched fists, she set a slow but determined pace toward the end. As she neared the point, she slowed. She could now hear the faint sound of falling water—a waterfall perhaps in the darkened distance.

"All the way to the point," Connell said.

"Of course," Helen grumbled softly as she continued away from the only torch near her.

But as she neared the end of the point, Helen noticed that, somehow, it was becoming brighter. So bright in fact, she had to shield her eyes. But just as she did, most of the brightness faded just as quickly as it came. In its place, now stood a lady on the point, just five paces from where she was standing. Looking to be in her late thirties or so, her complexion was flawless, her ears pointed, and her hair lay upon her back, long and blonde. Her smile seemed as warm and friendly as her blue eyes.

"I didn't have to call your name," Helen mumbled.

"What is my name?" the Lady asked.

"Lady Andrea Amora," Helen answered with a bow.

The Lady's smile widened. "Bright Helen." She gave a slight bow as well. "These, your gifts, are almost my last charge. I have only one other before I can go. It pleased me when I heard the Wizard

Andsell had set your path before me. It also pleased me that he had chosen a young girl to carry on in his stead."

"Thank you," Helen said with a slight courtesy. "He has sent me to collect a stone. Are you to help me with that?"

The Lady looked toward the sleeping Dragon and then back to Helen. "Among other things," she added. She then turned and held out her hand toward the sound of the waterfall.

Little by little, Helen's attention was drawn to something floating toward her from the darkness. Easing closer to the bank, she spotted a little, cedar boat slowly making its way in her direction. But it contained not a soul. Standing as still as her excitement would allow, she watched it nose upon the rocks just a short reach from her.

"Your turn, Bright Helen," Lady Amora said. She then nodded toward the little boat, still holding its place at the bank.

Helen looked back at the Lady. She gave a weak nod toward the little boat.

Leaning a bit forward, Helen could see two things inside the little craft. One, the larger of the two, was in the bottom of the boat and directly in front of its only seat. Wrapped in a dark, lavender blanket trimmed with a satin edge of the same color. What it covered looked to be the size of a football, but a little bigger. The other was wrapped in brown suede, tied with a blue ribbon, and rested above it on the top of the seat itself.

"The blue ribbon first," Lady Amora suggested.

Helen gently pulled the little boat more up on the bank and then gingerly stepped inside. Quickly untying the smaller package, she slowly unfolded the leather to find an oval shaped stone. It was a light green color and about the size and shape of a hen's egg. She quickly looked back at Lady Amora.

"That is the stone of Arvin Morrell," she said. "He was a good friend to your grandfather Andsell and a Green Wizard of worth." She stepped closer to Helen, now still in the boat. "Keep it safe. Your staff now rests in its sheath upon the Dragon. Now, be careful and pick up your second gift. Bring it before me and place it at my feet."

Helen quickly put the leather wrapped stone in her pocket with the blue ribbon and then gingerly picked up the other gift.

"It's warm," Helen said softly. As she carefully stepped from the boat, she looked at Lady Amora. "What is it?" she asked.

Lady Amora's smile widened. "The last of its kind," she replied. She stepped closer to Helen and then added, "Place it upon the floor before me. I would see it one-last-time."

Feeling the warmth within the blanket, Helen walked slowly toward Lady Amora. But just as she bent down to put it upon the floor, something jerked within the tightly folded blanket.

Helen quickly stood, still holding the object within the blanket. Looking at Lady Amora, she said, "Something moved within the blanket, My Lady."

"Indeed, it did move," the Lady of the Lake replied. She stepped closer to Helen and then carefully unfolded the 'gift' still in her arms.

Helen's eyes grew big as she looked at the tan, oval-shaped object. "It's still very warm," said Helen. "Is this what I think it is?"

Lady Amora smiled as she stood there looking back at Helen. "I can do a great many things, Bright Helen, but I cannot read your mind," she said softly.

"Omega!" Pragamore called, still lying close to the fire.

"Omega?" Helen looked toward the Dragon.

The huge Dragon nodded. "When the young one before you comes into this world, she will be called Omega. She is of my blood, the last of my seed, and the last of the Lake."

"Oh…my…God," Helen stammered as she looked back at Lady Amora. "We have yet another Dragon?"

"Truly the last," Lady Amora replied. "Providing you with the crystal and the egg is but one of two of my last charges from the Lake of Mirrors. The Stone of Arvin Morrell and Omega are now in proper hands. Go now, take the 'child' to Pragamore, and then put the stone at the head of your staff. Guard them both well."

"Thank you," Helen said as she slowly backed from her with a slight bow.

"You are welcome," the Lady said. "But remember, the gift within the blanket is not yours yet. Your 'gift' will be the honor of raising the 'child'. See that your course is well set."

"I will." Helen covered the egg with the blanket and then looked back to Lady Amora.

"You, yourself, are very young," the Lady added. "But then again, so was Richard at this point. Time will catch up to you quickly I believe. Now, like I said, go and place the child before Pragamore and place your stone at the head of the Staff of Bumpus."

~ * ~

Still standing at the entranceway, Glain and the others watched as Helen walked away from Lady Amora, and went straight to Pragamore.

"Did she get the stone?" Pereen whispered.

"What is she carrying?" Connell asked.

"Shhh!" Glain hissed. "She's laying something in front of Pragamore. "Maybe we can hear what is said."

~ * ~

Helen walked over to the seemingly sleeping Dragon and placed her hand upon his head. "Pragamore..." she said softly. "Lady Amora said you should see." Helen gingerly unfolded the blanket. "This is your child, Omega."

~ * ~

"Child?" With a strong grip on Glain's shirt, Connell eased herself and him from the group. She stopped at the head of the way to the point, watching closely.

~ * ~

"It needs your warmth, Pragamore," Helen said as she unfolded the blanket.

"Remove the blanket," the Dragon said weakly. "It needs more than my warmth."

Helen's chin slowly dropped as she did what she was told. Slowly standing, she asked, "Are you all right? Your voice sounds a bit weak."

"Never better than right now, My Lady," the Dragon answered. He raised his head and looked down at the egg.

He then blew a long, slow torrent of hot air toward the egg causing it to move about slightly. In doing that, he lowered his head toward the egg. When but a hand's distance away, a bright blue bolt shot from the nose of the Dragon only to disappear into the egg.

Pragamore then looked at Helen. "As I have said—the child will be called Omega. She is truly the last Dragon of the Lake of Mirrors."

~ * ~

"Goodness," Connell said still near the entranceway. She clutched

Glain's arm tightly. "That is a Dragon's egg she was given."

~ * ~

Helen, still standing at Pragamore's side, pulled her staff from the sheath beside the Dragon's saddle and placed the stone within its silver hand. As soon as the stone was seated, movement on the lake caught her eye. Slowly moving away from the Dragon and the fire, she saw two objects walking on the water toward the darkness.

"Lady Amora?" she called weakly.

But the figures did not stop, nor did they acknowledge her call. One was definitely Lady Amora, but the other walking beside the Grand Elf was much too large to be a person. Then, remembering Lady Amora said she had one, last charge, Helen gasped.

"Pragamore!" She gasped as she wheeled and looked back at her old friend.

But now, he was not alone. He was being attended by four Dwarves. They looked to be quickly taking the saddle from him. He looked asleep, but he didn't move at all.

"Pragamore!" she screamed as she ran toward the Dragon and those working around him.

"He is but asleep!" Helen pleaded. "Put the saddle back on him! He will need it to return with us."

"Now, now, Lass," one rather heavy-set Dwarf said as he took her in his strong arms.

"Pragamore!" Helen screamed again as tears burst forth and ran down her cheeks. "He can't be…" She looked at the Dwarf who held her tightly. "Gremniss, He can't be truly gone?" she pleaded.

"He is, My Lady," the Dwarf said. "He passed knowledge to the child, laid his head upon her blanket, and then passed from this realm." Looking back at the others, he added, "Take the saddle to the Old One! Tell him all went as expected."

Helen pushed and pulled herself away from Grimness and ran toward the Dragon. Stopping at Pragamore's head, she fell to her knees, gently stroking it and sobbing. She glanced back at Gremniss, now standing very close to her. "The Lady said she had one more charge," Helen sobbed. "But I didn't realize what it was. I didn't understand it." She eased her head to the Dragon's neck and continued to weep."

Glain, easing up beside Helen, helped her to her feet. "It's time you gathered your charge to you, My Lady. You are a parent now and you'll need some help with this. There is none better than the Elf, Prone Gerlinn. When she finds out there is yet another Dragon to be raised, she will be more than happy to come back with us I'm sure. She's a wiz with animals and has worked with Dragons in the past."

"Move to the door, Lass," Gremniss said as he handed Helen the lavender blanket. "It won't take but a minute ta catch."

"Let's go," Connell said as she gently placed a hand on Helen's back. "Hold tightly to that egg. Glain will help Grimness with what needs be done."

As they neared the entranceway, Helen looked back to check on Pragamore one, last time. When she did, she saw Glain and the Dwarf prodding at the fire with long poles. As the logs broke from the burning pile, they were rolled to the Dragon's side.

"Oh please…" Helen begged as she, once again, sank to her knees.

"I've got you! I've got you!" Connell said as she grabbed Helen and the egg and went to the stone floor with them both. "This is the way," Connell explained. The Dragon Pragamore is no longer with us. The methane within the Dragon's system is seeking a way out even now. It won't take long. Watch and learn."

Helen slowly shook her head. "I cannot," she whispered. "He is no longer there is he?"

Pereen slowly shook her head. "No my dear. He is still here, but worlds away as well. He watches."

Then, as the Dragon's fire started burning very brightly, the whole cave started to shake and groan.

"Glain!" Connell shouted from the entranceway. "We have to go now! The lake is starting to pour from its banks!"

"She's right," Gremniss agreed. He and Glain quickly threw down their poles and ran for the entranceway. "This place sounds like some great giant waking from a deep sleep.

"It's not 'waking'," Connell said. "It's about to leave all of us and I don't want anyone to go with it."

Without another word, Glain quickly led Connell, Helen with her egg, Pereen, and Gremniss out of the cave and toward the buildings. As they did, the stone walkway began to crumble under their feet, causing several to stumble.

Hearing the noise, Helen slowed and looked back. "Oh…my…

God," she groaned as she watched great stones, seemingly pulling themselves free of the cliffs above the opening. They then slid down and filled the yawning entranceway to the Cave of Mirrors. Water, still spilling from the entrance, was fighting its way between the stones that now blocked the entrance blocked.

"What's happening to it?" Connell asked.

Glain slowly shook his head as he encouraged Helen to continue. "The world of men is drawing nearer. Time has now caught up with this once wonderful place," he said as he stopped the little group at the buildings and then looked back at the happening.

Huge billows of steam were now pouring through the stones that now blocked the cave's entrance, but the water had ceased, leaving the walkway completely covered.

"Your dragon! Your dragon!" an elderly man shouted, leading a small group up the pathway and toward them. "Will not he be trapped?"

With all the excitement, the little group refused to get close to Glain and his group.

"He is no longer there," Helen said as she gently stroked the egg. "He is about to be reborn to us."

~ * ~

Helen remained strangely quiet during the plane ride back to Safe Haven. She continually pulled the blanket back and looked at what she now referred to as "the miracle within the blanket". At times, she seemed to be silently crying. The tears dripping from her chin gave her away. With Pereen and Connell constantly consoling her, she finally drifted off to sleep.

~ * ~

Finally, around 2:30AM that morning, a series of bumps jarred Helen awake. Gently holding to the egg, she looked out to see a grassy field passing before her window and the familiar beacon fire at the end of the runway. A short distance away stood a lady, waiting patiently.

"That's the Elf, Prone Gerlinn," Glain said, glancing back at Helen.

"She takes care of animals and such here at Safe Haven," Connell added. "She knows and is very excited about the 'gift' you now have within the blanket."

As soon as it came to a stop, the Elfin lady walked briskly toward the plane. Looking in her fifties, the trim, sandy-haired lady stopped right at the plane's door and opened it.

"We must be careful," she said, looking straight at Helen. "I am Prone Gerlinn of Safe Haven. "I have actually known the Dragon Pandahar as well as your Pragamore. You are Bright Helen aren't you?"

Helen, holding to her seat as well as the egg, nodded slightly as she took note of the Elf's pointed ears and greenish eyes. But her smile seemed as genuine as her excitement. "I don't feel very bright right now."

Prone, with a slight smile, nodded. "May I help," she asked softly as she extended her hands toward the blanket.

Helen looked down at what she was holding and then back up at Prone. "Very well," she finally said, then eased the 'gift' toward the Elf.

"I got him," the Elf said softly.

"Him?" Helen frowned.

"Just guessing," Prone said with a slight smile.

"Her name is Omega," Helen said. "Pragamore named her just before his spirit left us. Lady Amora said she was female."

"Oh…my…word as an Elf," Prone said, looking down at what she was holding. "A female Dragon we have here? The Lady of the Crystal Cave told you?"

"Pragamore," Pereen said as they stepped out of the plane."

Prone's chin dropped slightly, and her gaze focused on Pereen. "Pereen Willingham…" she said softly. "I should have guessed a White would be with the 'child'."

"It's almost three in the morning," Glain said. "We will rest here. I don't feel we should push on right now. We still have two thirds of the trip before us."

"Then stay with us," Prone suggested. "We have a small building ready just in case. I'll rouse you at nine or so and make sure you have a good meal for the trip." She looked hopefully at Glain.

"That's awfully decent of you," Connell said.

Glain stepped closer. "There is one other favor I would like to tempt you with."

Prone's eyes widened. Her gaze went from Helen, to the 'child', and then ended up on Glain. "And that would be…"

"We desperately need your help," Connell said.

Prone's smile widened as she looked down at the still covered 'gift' in her arms. "I suppose you do, don't you?" she finally said. "If it's about taking care of what I am now holding, I don't need to be paid. I would do it for the honor of it all and room and meals as long as I am allowed to stay." She then looked at the 'child' and continued. "I was but a child when Kraiton served the Wizard William. Then, there was the Dragon Pandahar with the Wizard Benjamin. When a young Richard rose to lead Whitestone, he raised his Dragon Pragamore from the very place this Child just came from." She looked at Helen. "Now, I am privy to be here and witness yet another binding."

"Binding?" Helen immediately looked at Pereen.

"Simple contact," Prone explained, looking at Helen. "Through Old Phagan, Pragamore and Lady Amora afforded you the opportunity no one else will ever have—the chance to have a symbiotic relationship with the last Dragon any of us will ever know again."

"Omega?" Helen's voice was weak.

"Of course," Prone replied. "When the Lady of the Lake handed you the egg in the lavender blanket that old geezer gave her, this wee 'child' felt your touch and probably moved. She knows you, Bright Helen, but the bond comes when it is hatched. She will seek you out. Even though she doesn't know what you look like, she will know who you are the moment she lays eyes upon you. She will stand very still right in front of you. Then, you must touch her. On the head perhaps would be good."

~ * ~

The next day, a Thursday on the twentieth day of April, Glain held the Beechcraft on a north-easterly course. Straight above the Green River he went where it bordered the Black Forest.

Pereen watched Prone closely. Several times she leaned close to the window, pondering the dense woodland passing beneath the plane.

"Something bothering you?" Pereen asked.

"Not sure," Prone said. "I had this uneasy feeling of dread just wash over me. For the like of me, I can't put a finger on from where it comes."

"Ghosts," Pereen said, laughing at the expression on Prone's face. "That's the Black Forest we're over right now. The Witches of Cromelea use to run a colony right there. When they attacked one of Old Benjamin's friends, he went into a rage and sent his Dragon Kraiton to destroy them."

"My word," Helen said as she also looked down upon the forest and then back at the 'child' in her arms. "I am feeling this as well—dread, hate, fear, and evil. Somewhere within that forest is where the Hagstorms and their riders once lived."

"The Hobuerich," Glain said.

"And the man who was after Pragamore," Pereen added.

Helen nodded. "That would be James Torrance."

"Great Gods!" Prone exclaimed as she sank back in her seat and closed her eyes. "What wickedness comes this way now?"

Helen looked at Pereen as if for answers.

"Don't look at me," Pereen said. "I don't know much about this man. "From what I am hearing, I think Pragamore should have ended him at the Big River. The Dragon, himself, said he should have killed him. Remember when he kidnapped the little Dwarf, Splinter. He left his friends to die in his place."

"Sounds just like him," Prone said.

Now, all in the plane were looking at the Dragon Keeper, hoping she could add something about Scar.

"How is it you know this man?" Pereen asked.

Prone shrugged. "Don't really know him. I just know of him," she admitted. "His full name is James Torrance Wharmod, a blond-headed, blue-eyed, Russian sorcerer and Wizard wan'na be. He has some kind of obsession with the Wizard Phagan's family. I hear the girl, Janice Dunn, is still having trouble with the man." She looked directly at Glain. "The 'child' and Helen are both young and weak compared to the likes of him. Pragamore was her strength. But now, he is no more. She will need help from us all, especially a wizard."

Glain rested deep back in his seat and then glanced back at Prone. "I teach and no longer do," he said. "I'm almost as old as Phagan."

"Nonsense," Prone grumbled. "You don't look a year over fifty to me. You helped defeat the one who ruled over those forests back there. For goodness sake, you were taught by Old Benjamin himself, the very one who taught Richard of Whitestone. You're a...a..."

"Wizard?" Helen guessed, now staring directly at Glain. "You can't be that old," she added with a bit of a squint.

Glain shrugged, trying to hide his amusement. "Connell has done her best to wash from me what she could of Fredwyn's curse. But youth and the Raven are still with me. Fredwyn wanted me to suffer as long as I could." His gaze slowly made its way to Helen. "I suppose Soot will have to serve yet another Wizard before my time is through."

Prone quickly moved to the front edge of her seat to better see Glain's expression. "Did I just hear a commitment?" she asked softly.

Glain smiled; but did little else.

"Glain Cerrig!" Prone called loudly. "You state your intentions this, very minute. Not a one of us can read your mind."

"I can," Helen said, her voice soft. "When you mentioned 'serve another Wizard', the 'child' within the egg moved.

Glain's smile widened. "That seals my direction," he said. "I am at your service as long as you need a worn out, old Wizard. But we must deal with a new enemy—one we know little of. The Sorcerer Wharmod will not stop. We do not know his strength, nor do we know how many are standing with him." He smiled at Helen. "I must fill the void Pragamore has left, find the sorcerer, and put an end to his devilment."

About the Author

M.R. Williamson was born on April 22, 1945, to a lower middle-class family on the outskirts of Memphis, TN. At that time, the 'baby boomers' were just budding into existence. His father's parents were a good part Native American of the Pawnee persuasion. They belonged to the Wolf-Cipi clan. His wife, Connie, has spent many long hours studying this genealogical question mark. Some of her studies have pointed her to Kansas with the names Two Shirts, Two Chiefs, Williamsons, and Russells.

Although his mother, Dorothy, was English and Scottish, his father, Russell, held fast to his Native American traits. The love of the woods, freedom, and nature were some of his strongest. These were surpassed only by the love he held for his family. M. R. has one brother, Ronald, and two sisters, Sandra and Tammy. Through his guidance, they were taught to love and respect every aspect of life. This was especially true for the 'little' ones of the wild. Because of this, and through his wife's understanding, M. R. has spent countless hours in the woods and on the waters. He has seen a number of things that would be, at least for him, hard to explain. He has always held a deep interest in the world of faeries and the mystical unknown. Some would call this fantasy or fiction, but there are those who would not.

As for M. R., he's never seen a dragon, nor had the pleasure of swapping stories with the fae people. He has, however, talked to a few rational people who have…according to them. His younger sister, Tammy, and her husband, Terry Barr, have also been severely bitten by this mythical bug. Terry, being a Tolkien expert, and an accomplished artist, has succeeded in fanning the flames of M. R.'s unyielding curiosity.

More books by M.R. Williamson from WolfSinger Publications

The Moleskin Cap

Helen is trying to get over the recent loss of her mother. Seeing the struggle, her father sends her to live with her grandparents. Now, among the forests her mother loved, Helen connects with her mother's hobby, photography. With her mother's first camera, an old Nikon, she snaps a shadowy figure in the early-morning shade of a fir tree. The resulting friendship not only pulls her from the destructive depression she was sinking into but leads Helen into a world of magic and adventure and gives her a new purpose in life and a new reason to live.

The Return of the Black Witch

One should not expect to slap the hand of an old crone and expect to walk away without at least a limp. The old witch Ethrel Ibenus is up to her tricks again and this time they've turned deadly. But where did her spirit go after Professor Martin shot her with his wee pistol?

Now, all are looking for the crone's familiar, Seleene. But the big timber wolf cannot be found. The search for the spirit of Ibenus now begins in earnest. Will Entwhistle and her Dwarves be able to help? Perhaps the Green Witch Pereen will be able to use a crystal derived from one of the Witch's own spells will do the trick. Fearing failure, Entwhistle improvises a plan 'C', the use of a mythical creature once thought to be long dead.

More Books from
WolfSinger Publications

The Steel Fist – Rob Jackson

The survivors of Recon 9 are needed in the Ozarks where some home-grown autocrats have taken over parts of Arkansas and Missouri. They've looted National Guard armories and hoarded weapons, ammunition, and vital supplies, just waiting for the opportunity to take over the area. While most of their transport, armor, and aircraft are obsolete, they face people with no protection against such deadly equipment. And they're trying to get the local natural resources to gain control of weapons even the military have no defense against.

Recon 9 has gained four new members and formed an alliance with locals, many of them veterans, against a common enemy. The locals have some grasp of tactics, an excellent knowledge of the hilly, forested countryside and a burning desire to be rid of the terrorists, who call themselves: THE STEEL FIST

Crisis in Big-G City – S.D. Matley

Olympus, Inc., is locked in battle with climate change!

Athena's Secret Ops program steps in when bad boy and technological genius Hermes can't come up with a carbon-curbing solution. Undercover agents Cleo Petra and Pan are deployed in the mortal world to vanquish the notorious East brothers, chthonic fossil fuel magnates who pass as human and eat humans, too…

Two-month-old Pablo, the one-quarter chthonic infant son of two fathers formerly known as P.B., employs his extraordinary abilities of adult speech and intellect in pursuit of climate justice!

Meanwhile, David Bernstein, whose hot romance with Cleo Petra meets a rocky end, recovers the memory of his century-old love affair with a beautiful Spanish nurse. He time travels to 1918 to find her and encounters love, loss, and the City of Mount Olympus

—a dark and sinister place where every inhabitant lives in fear of volatile and destructive Zeus!

David's birth father and Hera's former fling, Saul Crispin, is outed as a mortal made immortal. Will Hera's high crime of granting Saul eternal life land her before a jury of her peers for judgment?

And what of baby-crazy Queen of the Underworld, Persephone, pregnant at last but not by Hades?

Intrigue, espionage, crimes of passion, secret babies and looming existential threats—everywhere you look there's a Crisis in Big-G City!

Tree of Bones – Book Two: A Familiar's Tale
- Verna McKinnon

Two Curses

A curse of Darkness… Deep within the Thill forest, stands a tree made of human bones, crowned in black leaves and red thorns.

A curse of Light… Beneath the Wastelands of Skarros, a crystal imprisons a dark, immortal queen.

The Sorceress, Runa, is tormented by horrific images of this tree of bones in a distant, lifeless forest. Even as the visions debilitate her, Mellypip, her beloved familiar, also experiences these sinister dreams, bound by the same dream seer magic as his mistress. The tree of bones summons Runa, and she must risk madness and death as obsession drives her on. What she finds reveals a devastating truth.

Koll the Sorcerer awaits trial for his crimes. His familiar, Xabral, searches for allies to free him. Driven by his own dreams of dark prophecy, Koll seeks to free Obsydia, the Bloodstone Queen, from her prison. Determined to let nothing stop him, Koll will commit any evil to achieve his goal.

Runa and Mellypip's newest journey reveals truths behind ancient secrets, as Koll's obsessive hunt for a fallen queen threatens to doom the world forever. Runa and Koll, bound by opposing magical destinies of Light and Dark, will ultimately face frightening revelations and unimagined consequences.

Gate of Souls – Book One: A Familiar's Tale
- Verna McKinnon

Familiars.
Magical animal companions of sorcerers.
Keepers of spells and secrets.
Most important, devoted friends for life.

When one such familiar, Mellypip, bonds with the young sorceress Runa, he shares in the wonders of magic. Together, Mellypip and Runa train under the tutelage of Runa's grandfather, Cathal, and his cantankerous mountain owl familiar, Belwyn. But secrets and spells do not make for good sorcery. Old friends begin to vanish even as enemies from Cathal's past return, threatening to reveal the truth of Runa's parents; a truth from which Cathal must protect his granddaughter at any cost. When Cathal is kidnapped, Runa and Mellypip rush against time to save their family and friends from dark sorcery that will not only destroy them, but shatter the Gate of Souls and release demonic creatures of The Otherworld into the mortal realms.

The Seven Exalted Orders – Deby Fredericks

Arkanost has Seven Exalted Orders. No more, no less. When a magus goes renegade in a far-off province, the Mage Lords demand something be done.

Ryamon is bitter and frustrated. He longs to be a Fire magus; as a Stone magus, he's miserable. If he can bring the rogue back, he has a chance—his last chance—to fulfill his dream.

It's a great plan—until he actually meets Valdira.

Tails from the Front Lines 2: The Thin Blue Line – edited by Carol Hightshoe

Come meet some of the four-legged members of Law Enforcement who also serve and protect.

Here our authors will introduce you to the brave K9 officers who serve alongside their human partners. They are their eyes, ears, noses and sometimes when necessary they are their shield, protecting others.

Proceeds from this anthology will be donated to the El Paso County (Colorado) Sheriff's Office K9 program in memory of K9 Jinx who was killed in the line of duty on April 11, 2022.

Ring of Fire – edited by Dana Bell

Enter the Ring of Fire, as unpredictable as the land masses shaking a city and volcanoes erupting covering the landscape. Could there be other reasons for these events? Or could these rings be more than a geological location.

They may be dragons playing tricks
or magic portals opened to mysterious realms
or sacrificing the best work of a lifetime.
Perhaps a rescue during a forest fire
or an attempt to raise the dead
or even while attending a high school reunion.

Journeys are taken to far off lands, another world, and through caves, each with their own unique twist.

Each tale presents a new idea on what the Ring of Fire could be. It is more than what many have been led to believe. Pull up a chair and warm yourself by our fires—just don't let yourself get burned.

Coyote – Charles Combee

While camping in a remote canyon in Utah Jim accidently sees an ancient rite taking place with a coyote like creature presiding over it. Now this creature wants Jim dead.

Audrey and her family go hiking in Utah and are attacked by this creature. Audrey is the only survivor, but she is pulled into a strange world of darkness and glass. She is 'rescued' by Jim, but is still linked to the creature, whose hold on her will end in her death unless Jim can find a way to break that link.

In his dreams, or are they ancient memories, Jim begins to learn more about Coyote as well as the magics that previously bound him. But those dreams end without teaching him the full magics. Can he find a way to free Audrey and stop Coyote from once again terrorizing humankind?

Believing is Seeing – Joanna Michal Hoyt

What we believe shapes what we see. Sometimes the stories we tell free us. Sometimes they trap us.

Some people see things their neighbors can't or won't see. Are they inspired? Delusional? Who decides?

As the faithful people of her village cry out for their god's help in disaster, a young peasant woman faces the terrifying possibility that she may be that god.

A time-traveling Jewish refugee visits 21st-century churches and confronts almost unrecognizable versions of himself.

Three troubled people make the dangerous visit to The Library where the maddening stories lodged inside them can be removed—on certain demanding conditions.

Having been warned away from the vacant lot which is said to house a portal to Hell, the new girl in town naturally goes to investigate.

Early in the grid collapse—or apocalypse?—a Christian lesbian farm couple paint "WELCOME" on their barn and await visitors.

An old man in the Terran diaspora enlists in a crusade to save humanity and belatedly wonders if he's on the wrong side.

Step inside these stories and see what you believe—but don't believe everything you see.

Out of the Darkness – edited by Carol Hightshoe

Mental Health issues have long been stigmatized, with those facing them pushed into the shadows, often unable to deal with the darkness they find themselves trapped in.

In this collection, stories explore many types of darkness—Suicidal Ideation, Death from Suicide, Survivor's Guilt, PTSD, Chronic Pain, Chronic Illness, Depression, Death of a Loved One, Secrets, Bullying, and other forms of darkness are explored. Some related to mental health issues and some not, but all of them offer very human perspectives. As in real life, some stories have happy endings and sadly others don't.

We offer these stories of darkness without judgement, but with hope and compassion. Some roads should never have to be traveled —but we understand that for many they are being traveled alone.

Proceeds from sales of Out of the Darkness will be donated to the American Foundation for Suicide Prevention—or more information on AFSP please visit their website at: afsp.org.

Never Cheat a Witch – edited by Carol Hightshoe

Magical curses. Arcane revenge. Being transformed into a frog. Things evil witches do to mere mortals who cross their path. But, what if there is more to the story…

Deals made with a witch are magically binding and can bring dire consequences to those who even think about breaking them.

Whether they are seeking revenge for wrongs done to them, helping others or simply trying to live their lives—it is NEVER wise to try and cheat a witch.

Open your spell book and join our authors as they relate tales of witches and mortals. From classic fantasy witches to modern day witches and even the legendary Baba Yaga. Good and Evil as well as every shade of gray in between.

And, yes—there is a prince who is turned into a frog.

And more – check out our books at

www.wolfsingerpubs.com